QUERENCIA
AUTUMN 2024

QUERENCIA

Querencia Press – Chicago Il

QUERENCIA PRESS
© Copyright 2024

ISBN

978 1 959118 42 8

.

www.querenciapress.com

First Published in 2024

**Querencia Press, LLC
Chicago IL**

Printed & Bound in the United States of America

CONTENTS

POETRY

Mother Magnified – LindaAnn LoSchiavo (she/her)

My mother's lies propelled her life, steered fate towards brittle stars. Truth, like silence, lodged itself like a bone in her throat.

It was my mother who marked the start of when my life was being archived. According to her, everything was my fault. Such distorted recollections became a burden, a sour aftertaste. A child, I sensed danger everywhere as she deftly plucked my words from the air and flung them back at me, keeping a straight face. Sharp was the taste of her rage, the biting sting of blood inside my cheek. The hidden weight of her weather oppressive, my secret self divulged little lest thunderbolts quake.

Eventually, I became a vegetarian, refusing to eat anything that had a mother. The slimmer I got, the more years my mother shaved off, making *herself* younger. An alibi saved for a day of need.

As maturity moved forward, the muscularity of forgetfulness tried to put its seductive palms on my lips and press down. Even imagination threatened to betray me, failing to make good on the fancies I'd hope to invent. But pen and paper became the dependable parents I'd always longed for. With them, I sketched realities I could eventually escape to.

Then along came cancer's onslaught, a beast that called to me like the wilderness summoned the pioneers. From the waiting room, I watched as she was wheeled into a bright cold room on a gurney whose wheels chattered despair. Surgeons promised to extinguish the embers of disease, snuff out its sparks, stamp it out. If the ending was good, it cast its goodness back on the whole like a beautiful sunset's crown after a storm.

Remission repainted the daylight a kinder shade, hinting at a longer stay. But in the rasp of her breathing, death listened for its cue like a stage-door Johnny.

Her final bout with cancer made her reconsider falsehoods that would be etched in tombstone cursive. Framing it as a wish to leave a place where bad luck cursed her, she offered her body to the incinerator, hoping to spell her body into stardust as bald truth, an unruly guest, would be escorted from the premises.

Bad memories are cadavers that refuse burial. Instead of an archive of velveteen nostalgia, her name leaves gravel in my mouth. But there is a dimension where regret might slumber as the sky offers continuity, its sonata of stars promising relief—light's unsingable psalm.

Upstairs – Liam Chimba (he/him)

He told me to lead with my knees.
I thought it was inappropriate.
What if my mask slipped and a part of me was exposed?

A shopping bag carrying stomach acid,
A window frame shaped like a cross,
The judges face staring back.

There was no love like hate, no hate like love,
No curtains on the house opposite us.

People spilled into each other,
Private little Luther's,
On their hands and knees,
Crawling through the window, through me.

I should care about who goes upstairs,
And in what order.
But I was made to go down,
The apples and pears.

is it really a twin flame or an abusive relationship? – tommy wyatt
(he/they)

your exlover as a solar flare or twin flame, they're all the same
when TikToks cluster in the refraction of your retinas, the field
of space comprised in breaks of time you think are quantum
shifts. if you blink hard enough, reality purges itself of scalar

magnitude, as you're consuming warm frequencies and
waiting for a plug to ply you full of ketamine you can't afford—
how will you get by when you're stunlocked from manifesting,
sourced back to the day you met, just to do it all over once more,

all high off sun and wanting to love because it's the only thing
convincing you to live? that viral 10-second clip will form a
mirrored you, unmeasured by trauma or reflecting your exlover, if
you can answer: what makes you think you'll ever want to live
again?

Five Ways to be Carried Away by the Devil. – Jessica Swanson (she/her)

Princess-style.
Hand about your waist.
Gently, gently. Weightless, sin upon sin.
I'll carry you myself. Heavy is the burden of an empty promise.
By violent surprise.
Affectionately, head over heels cliffside.
All this vertigo landscape could be yours:
a kingdom of rational 9-to-5's and privacy screens.
Desperately over the shoulder.
Pretend you've found a white-collar angel.
Someone to whisper bittersweet nothings, lost to the breeze at
your back, the hand trailing up your thigh.
Carelessly dangling.
Snatched claw-deep, bleeding memories of sleepover games.
All your friends chanting, "Light as a feather, stiff as a board."
Where is she now, waiting to move the planchette
and call you home?
On all fours.
Beast of burden, scratchy and glittering.
Horseless rider, this apocalypse takes a familiar shape.

(What do you go by now? What's your name? What should I call you?)

purity culture insisted I was inherently dirty – Ivy L. James (she/her)

It is 2006 and I am barely twelve years old and the youth pastor spits out a chewed-up wad of gum and tells me I am that gum if I let a boy touch me before marriage. I stare at the spearmint-green lump dented by molars. How could that be me? It is 2007 and I have finally made it to thirteen and this year the youth pastor stomps on a rose and tells me I'm the dirty shredded petals if I touch myself. It is 2008 and fourteen is a terrible thing to be and the youth pastor looks right at me with his latest metaphor and I am chewed up and stomped on and filthy and I am broken, I am broken, I am broken. It is 2012 and I am in college at sixteen, and in this moment in my dorm there is no youth pastor, there is no gum or rose or dollar bill or anything, it's just me and a sapphic fanfic and I'm realizing, now, in terror, why it was so easy to promise not to have sex with boys, why the purity ring slid so effortlessly onto my teenage finger: I don't *want* to have sex with them. It's women I'm interested in, but I run the risk of being expelled from church and school and family if I act on the attraction, so I hide. It is 2015 and I can drink now and I want to be fixed so I sleep with a man but it's nothing to me, it's bland compared to the relief of the Supreme Court case. It is 2017 and twenty-three is both old enough and young enough to reach for what I want, and my purity ring is gone, I don't know where, and I part my legs for a woman for the first time,

and I am pieced together.

Down, Down, Down - Paris Woodward-Ganz (he/him)

head and shoulders and knees, bruises
      like rotten plums on dark skin bursting

too big for my body. i hold sin in
      the back of my mouth, taste heavy

weight and regret and disgust on
      my tongue, forking between my teeth

like temptation. oh, tell me that i'm
      beautiful! november shatters like glass

in my soft mouth and your clock—
      hands grasp me like a ship about to dock.

take me to your shores, your body an
      island. there we're free from shame and

regret, touch my body like you want
      to burn me at the stake. oh call me

good please call me good i want
      to be your salvation. i can be a

boat or a blessing or nothing
      more than a body for you

to beat and to break but i can
      be good oh i want to be so good

it aches.

Between Two Spaces – Anam Tariq (she/her)
—after the strawberry moon of June '23

The moon in flames—
tawny, terra cotta, silent tones of a ripened autumn
overcome the satellite,
seeming a vintage Japanese lamp
releasing waves of vintage shades
at a high elevation.
I, capturing the curves in the cursive's careful twirls
as the river runs wild in horizontal lines
across the folio before me.
The lamp is burning high behind
forked trees
and crumpled thought balls are jarring behind
locked doors
but what matters now
is the warmth of the sifting moonlight
through the atmospheric layers,
collecting in the process
pieces of peace as the unspoken outside
hands down a secret to me.
Handing it down to my other friend,
with a home along the lines of paper,
with an equal share in this remedy,
ensues an engrossing discourse in verse
about the green spaces nesting
beyond our housed lives
in the branches of the planet
while the brain erases traces
of the scrunched-up trash(y thoughts)
taking up space back home.

grounded flights – Tanisha E. Khan (she/her)

on a chittagong rooftop beneath heat clogged skies,
I lay with my *nannu* on beach chairs, gazing
up at airplanes. the plate of cactus-cut
fries balanced on my belly a soother
for my discontent in your absence.

in our hushed, potted guava cocoon,
I unearthed my secret grievances:
I enjoy nothing when dad isn't home. nothing.
training on the other side of the
planet, I imagined you having fun without me,
riding merry-go-rounds and teacups,
throwing pounds of pennies into wishing wells,
making sundaes, seeing elephants at the zoo,
and telling someone else the tale
of a thousand thieves.

I did not understand your ambition—
the turning of pistons, goliath machines,
math problems the length of my arms—
how much this calling defined you.
on our walks through kirkland park, in toronto,
to distract me from the geese, you would point up
at a plane and say, *let's measure the distance
and angle between us and that little flier up there.*
I felt the oceans between keenly during your trips,
dreamt of you soaring over pacific waters, above
the cloud line, and still the fish were large enough
to snap at the wings. octopi tentacles snaked
around the plane's body, tugging it toward the
deep and squid released ink to make the pilot go
blind. I made mum phone you in the morning,

waking you from your jetlagged sleep, to hear

your voice. laughing, you reminded me that fish
can't reach planes. *what about blue whales?* I asked.
you chuckled; said you bought me sneakers that glow
in the dark, joked you would take me to the aquarium
after you flew back home.

now you grow vegetables in the backyard:
flowering purple cabbage, rigid celery stalks,
onions, speckled squash, striped zucchini—your
green fingers till the soil with mechanic precision.
for the past five years, you've sat on the old brown
couch in pursuit again, but with little luck, awe turned
to nightmare tentacles threading through you,
keeping you earthbound.

I feel the distance keenly, again;
no math problem enough to calculate
the depth of hurt, the fissures in your body from
years of the industry fracking you, your willingness
and wonder. airplanes are now the stuff of static life—
the trips not taken, the vacations missed, the visits
to grandparents made too late, and the need to
say no because there isn't enough...

still, sometimes you pause, look up at the sky and smile.
you ask, *can you measure the distance between you and the plane?*

Journey to the Center of God's Eye – Andrea Aldrete (she/her)

It's 4:28pm on a Thursday. Nothing special
about the mundane. Just a string of even
numbers flashing on a clock,
moments away from turning odd.
We are spinning on this wheel
and we never feel the Earth
shake. Save for the times
it almost kills us.
I can't help but think
it must be in vain. I never see it,
but I can almost taste it slip away.
We leave our mark before the rain.
Before the ages turn all that glitters
into rust.
It fades and so do we.
We carve out a piece
of something whole
and call it *holy*
only because our hands fail to tremble
when we hold it.
I left my heart in the blistering sun,
wet and beating, swallowed up
by fields and sky.

The soil is warm, the light is blinding,
and the heels of time keep digging
  and digging
    and digging
      and digging...

The Sapphic Is A Stanza For the Late Night Queer – Sammy Ismet Merabet (they/she/he)

Last month, I glanced down when a man called me a
whore as we stood waiting for our 1 A.M.
bus. My skirt—a floral and tattered rag that
let in the cold night—

didn't look at either of us. Instead, it
kept to my waist, holding on 'till I, fed up,
slipped it off and into my bag at my stop.
As if I had lost.

Walking back, I quickened my whore legs. It fell
out the bag as I sped up, tripping me, and
when I tried to pick it up it got caught and
tore under my shoe.

Tears in florals are to be expected, though.
Petals ripped by kids and their hands or me and
mine. Or yours. When Hyacinth tore, you stuck your
feminine finger

into his new laceration, and curled it.
Opened him more. Viscera flushed at your touch.
You felt boyish blood and a pistil warm and
loosen around you.

You made sense of anther and filament, style,
stigma. God, you thrive off of stigma. He tore;
you tore him more, fertilized him and his place.
Bloody and dirty.

Gods are great at bloody and dirty. You look
down at my skirt. Teased, it looks back up at you.
Tear it more. Please. Carefully. Make it whorish.
Visceral. Floral.

Narcissus – Divya Venkat Sridhar (she/her)

the stars are footnotes of the evening
and we are alone now, moments apart,
the pond searing lines into everything
that needs saying.
you reach
for my hand but press wrinkles
into it—an absent wound.
a pebble's reflection plops into
my screaming mouth
and my lips dance like smoke.
the moon spills over
your nose, bleeding
like a swollen tooth
in a shattered smile.
ripples thread into my hair
                          and so you wait
until the water forgets,
until it hardens into a poem
formless **flawless**
echoing your name, knowing
it has come long, so long,
just to touch my skin.

you can't stop it, it's a canon event – tommy wyatt (he/they)

gravel to digital sand[1]   crashwatching yourself
staring too long   lately do you ask
    how & not why
you can reach all the way   in & not feel
scared it's lagging   your body
a screen   all silvered out   & flashing
peppered with light   synthetic & nightwoozy
when you choose   to be more portal
than person   again &   again &   again
&

you can't skip over the bad parts without blankness
        you can't miss time quartzing to glitterynothing & see how
                you can't trick yourself into screenblinking away chances

to be more than static leeching your field of vision with pearlgray
so one-dimensionally girlsure & easy to dissect & pretty enough
to be cast in the background since you're bent on gendermoding
& cloaking yourself with the blurriness of it all when you know how
digitaltouch is never enough & soon sight will flux & still slowly for
you to know what's wrong with this image

---

[1] Inspired by "Starburned and Unkissed" by Caroline Polachek
from the *I Saw The TV Glow* soundtrack.

Halloween Baby - Noll Griffin (he/him)

If I'll be a ghost, I'll stretch into a speech bubble
floating above incredulous expressions
to back them up when they remember to say
the best comeback by the time the socializing ends,
with a gasp from the stiff back I wrapped in this sheet.
I'll cross my invisible arms around a sticker-studded urn
squeezing between two bottles of electric syrup
in the tasteful liquor cabinet that only made
the whole living room learn to sing.
I'll lure wild autumn rabbits under windows,
when the very way the sun comes says we've had enough,
with levitating scoops of rustled seeds in my elbow
to watch my favorite drowsy faces bloom at the glass
no matter how many future fruit salads get stolen
while I bend the broken stems into anklets,
another spirited act I'll have to sleep on.
I'll be more fun then as the paranoid pedestrian
watching temporary holiday shops
beg me to have a party big enough to keep them full.
I twitch off the mattress in a catalog dream of morbid costumes
for light occasions, my calmest grin under ill-fitting latex,
drapes flail across my bad dance moves in a misted mirror frame
to see which one could mend the funniest patch
over my awkward spot at a table that wants me, but
I'm so cold when I make do with one disguise.

Judge's scales – Liam Chimba (he/him)

They tore my mother open, rib to gleaming rib.
It was my fault.
And although they say that it's impossible,
I'm sure that I can remember it.
The scalpels clashing as they reflected hot blood,
cutting a smile into her ribcage.
Scarlet splashing on their beaks.
I was born from that hole in her stomach,
born watching her ribs flutter like centipede legs,
and I inherited that knowledge:
I was born from her ribcage,

Eating was not a question for me,
Just an art,
Saturn with his son,
My mother with her burden,
And the scale judging me; she always said I might shatter
Or she might shatter,
I can't quite remember.
But I can believe some things,
Cordless chargers, banned shoelaces,
Anti-rip bedsheets,
And the scale.

My father used to stir his tea,
He'd put the milk in first,
And as the water was boiling,
He'd tell me about Mbombo,
The God who'd float in a primordial river,
And, seasick, he started to heave,

And give birth to this world,
Another person I was not supposed to talk about,
Just live with,
Like his eyes were inside of me.

The Red Egg – Katie Beswick (she/her)

For years, in a suitcase in my shed,
an egg nestled among so many stolen eggs.
The egg was speckled with dots of red.

Inside the egg, universes bled;
curdled scarlet, gelatinous time, stretched—
things you said and never, never said.

Lambswool cushioning for a bed.
Quick stealing fingers, pinching, pinching eggs.
An egg of blood rolled, egg-shaped head.

Peeling paint peels, paper shreds.
Stars burst hotly, shooting sky cracked egg,
and wrought in claret a road ahead.

I turn it over: red, red egg.
Feel its burn against my leg—
then lock it back up in my shed.

jan. 2009 - Layne Joy Ruda (she/her)

The first time J kissed me was
under a streetlamp. He unveiled a pool of
acacias and shamrocks and we dove in,
floated, grasped for one another blindly.
See, the deeper we swim,
the muddier our memories. I've lost
sight of the playground equipment at 1am, but
I can feel the phantom swing set seat on
the backs of my thighs as we bask under the streetlamps,
stomachs full of day-old cinnamon rolls, and I jump.
We are crafted from cement chips of
the streets we sauntered. See, the deeper we swim,
the sooner we erode, but there will always be
splinters of us. My name is spelled out
where the light meets the street—
a balmy, January sunset   birthing,

                                        crawling to a dry.

timonium / elysium – Natalye Childress (she/her)
—after edgar kunz's "dundalk"

it happened on a weekend, and before the monday morning bell rang, the news had made the rounds. in the driveway, at the high school, there were tears, reporters. there was disbelief. a boy like that, one from the suburbs—the way-out ones, not the first-ring ones—you don't expect him to cause any trouble. in dundalk, lansdowne, maybe. but not here, where the master masons and eastern stars come to die. *these kinds of things don't happen here.* suburb boys don't shoot up, they just shoot guns. and that boy is hot-blooded like a horse, like the thoroughbreds running furlongs in late august. a year later and he's just begun his first two life sentences. another fifteen years pass before i find myself at the scene of the crime. i'm calculating half-lives, trying to make sense of it, knowing not everything has an explanation. that night, i walk the inner harbor, imagining the twinkling lights just out of frame to be the key bridge, a cathedral enshrining the patapsco. in one month, it'll be another site marking where people died, a half-finished palace, an immortal's resting place. floating cranes and hydraulic grabbers will dismantle the wreckage. the army will come in and blow it up. now, there are reroutes and slowdowns. a man sits in standstill traffic in the harbor tunnel 50 feet under. his commute has doubled overnight. in the backseat, his young daughter wonders why she can't see the water encompassing the tube. if she concentrates hard enough, she can see through the concrete and into the green backwater. she can see the bonejack, the blueback, the alewife, the vampire fish, the tide covered with froth. she can see into the sky, into space, the valleys on mars not all that different from the rivers on earth.

Dumpling girl - Jong Yun Won (he/him)

she's not actually made of dumplings
but she does have a philosophy:

to make one thousand good Dumplings
by the time she dies, one for each person she loves

she's in the process of making one now
folds every crimp oh so nicely
stuffs it with her beads, her beautiful fillings

each Dumpling is a metaphor for
flour on a kitchen island
swirls of oak and jade

the sun shining in the shape
of your favourite white lady
at the farmer's market—

before it hits the steamer, I snatch the dough
and smush it.

Dumpling girl slaps me with the might
of her Aunties, one of whom is Shakira
yes, her Auntie is Shakira

she returns for another Dumplingbowl
halftime, holds a singing dumpling in the air.

I'm sorry. You're right.
This is dumplinghood.

My male relatives would never touch the dough.

Show me how you made that again
each rung you folded was sturdy
built to hold a warm center.

Poem about - Allison Thung (she/her)

I. No one

All I have remaining of you is the belief that I have anything remaining of you.

II. Nothing

Perhaps the only time there was a point at all was at the very start, but only for an instant, before it meandered into a perpetual line that ends only when I stop drawing it out.

III. Nowhere

The worst part is not the never-ending chase itself, but the lack of clarity on the purpose of the chase, such that all it becomes, is a run, from or to what also unknown, and god knows I'd rather miss a bus from *no-where* to *now-here* than run.

matins – Malachy Harris (they/she)

concrete grey   fuzz of the morning after
tiled bathroom white nineteen-seventies plastic fittings
black mould peeling caulk and fag stains
before the mirror he stands naked
        blade in hand.

the night before he
        crawled sifting and switching
through the rubble of the long-past
searching for something that
proved it not to be true

lifted by the folds   shaved arms
broad uncovered shoulders back
open your dark eyes wide and raise your orange eyebrows
don't interject
        whatever you do

razor shifts *purple blue green red pink* splits
reforms dead frizzled ends cuts back un-
smirks smiles grimace and pukes sick to her teeth
—wanted growth liberates and reveals

the bathroom remoulds itself
comedown—
        plasticene rainbows strewn colours ribbons of *purple blue
green red pink yellow* confetti explodes the night before
reaches for the box behind the mirror and

plastic strips of little white dots
carefully loaded into a pill-cutter
mushroom with the red divided   stored
one every eight

becoming   the gentle waking ritual
reforms and re-finds herself
clear in the stabilising mirror

Prometheus - Paris Woodward-Ganz (he/him)

one day you will become your destiny
    says the burning sky when the city falls to pieces,

shattering into ice blue shards
    and pottery fragments. *he will kill you*

my mother repeats, wrapping my wounds
    with a bloody bandage, peeling the scabs from

my purpled knees. i go back to the edge
    of the river and kneel, slipping my hands

into the dry riverbed, the heavy echo of
    hands on my hips enough to stir the salt

from its land-locked place in the brown silt.
    she stares and i say nothing, peeling orange skin into the dirt.

you never used to like that sweetness. she frowns and i hand
    her my pearly white childhood. I see my father standing on the other bank,

worrying the hole in his chest with shaky fingers.
    don't we like things differently at the end of the world?

she never answers me and the vision blurs and fades.
    i let my fingers drift below my belt, rind bleeding

beneath my nails. the riverbed becomes
    a night riddled with pox scars and blemishes,

a boy drowning in the sweetest music.
    white pearls crest, a neck learns to bear

the delicate noose of waves. suppose i was
    not every flame that people burned, a lit cigarette

kissing a collarbone like a bird's hollow wing.
    suppose i was my father's son and not an inferno,

a wildfire settling in my stomach along with the black
    daisy. i am every charred offering twisted under my fingernails.

i am every burning forest, the whistle of birdsong
    sinking into the stone, the wind stirring the summer

into a gaping wound. the orange rind slips open
    like a soft mouth, twilight fading into blue. the eagle perches again

on the hour and begins to cry. i can't tell you whether
    i loved the pain or just the desire. can you devour me like the wolf,

building rome out of my blood? when you peel
    my guts from my stomach can you still taste the ash?

vacation days - J M Roberts (she/her)

i. the birds

we will now be taking a quick commercial break.
look at these colors. taste the straws and bears
in the airs and something cries *where, where, where...*
do this, do that, then put it away. hand me the key.
hand it to me, like that, there. sit
and let it hang. let them all leave.

close your eyes.
now open. it all looks the same, doesn't it?
notice that the difference is what you think is happening.
there's nothing here, nothing outside of here,
notice that it's okay.

green pigment on these growing walls. view of the ocean sloshing
in its open basin below your cliff and you can hear the birds
they're sick and crying and you can stand at the closed window
where you barely have to listen. you see the warm tangerine radio
break waves on your arms, necks, chest, eyelids, yes you can see
it, everything you see is real, yes it is.

when we return to the program (in just a few minutes now,
don't worry, I'll let you know in advance), you will not be there.
I will be there, though.
I will tell you what I find, will bring you... what do you want?
a wristband with your name on it? a puzzle piece,
dropped by flightless birds the next world over, who knows
how they managed to get it here or why. does anyone know?

it all seems impossible to you, all of it
but you don't have to understand it. not
now. wouldn't it be awfully naive
if you thought you could?

ii. the jello

you want the jello, but you won't ask for it. you see him
there eating it in his chair he has stacked four cups
of jello on the table next to him. you wouldn't even eat it
if the nurses set it prettily before you so what's there
to indicate you want it? the idea, the belief?

the jello is the color of absinthe. the jello is not
a solid. the jello is a turtle lost its shell, still
warm tender beating. the jello, it's a muscle.
the jello is aware of this conversation right now. the jello
voted for Al Gore. the jello has a favorite movie.

you could eat it and then it would be inside you.
to some people it seems so simple an equation to
consume a body and keep it, but you know it's
more like quantum physics. it takes time and calculation to
make nice with the jello and introduce yourself carefully.

it's okay if the jello doesn't immediately warm up to you
or you need to step away. conversations
with jello (or any of its relatives) can be intense. so
take it slowly. breathe. that's it, breathe. when
you're ready, start from the top. tell it:

1. Your name
2. Your birthday
3. Your favorite color
4. Your pH balance (this might take some preplanning)
5. Your blood type
6. Your favorite film
7. Your favorite shade of green
8. Your most recent meals (jello can get along with any foods, it just
    needs time to prepare)
9. Any history of mental illness in the family
10. And ring size (these relationships can get serious, if it goes well)

be honest, above all. jello will know by the taste
of your saliva or the number of freckles on your nose today
if you're lying or holding anything back. and you know it knows,
doesn't it? don't you? look at these kelly green walls
frothy and raving. they wouldn't lie to you, would they?

iii. the book

There! There the stark unyielding of the plutonian landscape or so
he said, That's what he told you. You trust his words because
they're in print, although you couldn't tell us exactly what they
meant. He told you:

That divulging the electric scorch of a dark pressing cloud pressed
on the kid's chest on his head like a hat which his arms are too
short for the thunder of bodies kicking up war in their wake of a
stampede of mindless inertia stammering the plateaus of a red
planet too bathed in its own ideas which wind up in uneven winds
and then settle never to be touched again just like you and even
he has not observed them and neither have you. Somewhere,
sitting with your legs outstretched and your hands in the middle,
you are good, so he says. So the kid stands there as we watch him
stand here as the pounding kiss the highlands and ideas wreak
their havoc where they can while we watch and he watches and
he's so far away from the event horizon where events are
happening but as far as he is,
you are even farther. Do you even know where you are?

If you want to touch it, you have to slither. You have to crawl, you
have to cry. You have to discard all the metal, food, and water in
your pockets, pick up your legs and walk right out. You have to
find someone to come get you because it's too far to walk.

Here's your phone, here's your tampon and your wallet.
Here, your laces. Take your life and leave. Don't you want it back?
Aren't you glad we saved it for you?

trading rocks for pinecones - Tohm Bakelas (he/him)

Menacing clouds mixed

with sundowning smiles,

things are not going so

well. I try trading rocks

for pinecones, but kicking

them just doesn't feel the

same. Where do you go

when the graveyard is

filled and no one

picks up your

call?

Cherry Tree - John Eric Hamel (he/him)

Sculpted to a mushroom cloud, or Chinese bell,
Dense with blossoms, a ringing chamber of bees
In early, eager motion, as if spring
Would only be that day,
Or too soon tomorrow they flounder with the rest
Dizzy on the sidewalk having lost the way.
With water in unlikely places and no mind for birds
That take us out, it's no one's loss
That we have found our way. Come close
And enter our school in harvest now,
Hear attentive words put closely to work.
As during an eclipse, in strange silence,
The traffic sounds remote and hear
The few scattered voices in uncommon interplay,
In awe and laughter crisp and echoing clean.
Long and steadily the dark draws on,
And quick, complete, the dizzying light of day returns!

In the Wake – Cimmerian Urbanek (they/them)

"How hot is the
night"
in the room without doors
where the chickens scratch scaled
feet to operatic bars on the tin roof.

Jars of hen's teeth
mosquito's fat slick on the sides of baby bottles
rougarou shed mange scabs lining the cradle
The dirt from the hoof walls of a lame cauchemar
scattered in wet mounds on the tired sofa.

"Hast noticed the smell of earth."
it weaves past the tiles
it gathers behind the ice box
The air is redolent of the forgotten
the forgotten material beneath our feet
in the center of our cells
Astral projections generated by tracing the whorls
of our skin, the whorls of the wood, the spiral
galaxy of the temporal lobe.

But nothing has changed
in the room without doors,
and the smell drops out of our
nostrils,
rolls a bit, and then lies still

Static echoes through the bent antennas
lurching in all directions
tangled hopelessly like the antlers of a live buck
caught in the velvet snare of the antlers
of his dead rival.

Just like that, the stench of change
is transmitted
where the receiver threads through both my
armpits.
Bending me back, an abandoned bow
on the windowsill of the window that is boarded up
endlessly. Layer upon layer of old beams
from destroyed houses
Victims of God

"How hot was the night"
in the space beneath the satellites
in the cabin sinking
into the quagmire of the inexplicable.

"We killed a great serpent coming across the plains."
Slipping off the coils of his rattle,
each ring a
plummeting
No seeds inside—not a child's maraca—just blood
but when I set his body to
desiccate
under my bed. All that was
left
was a mass of old dandelion heads. A white
sausage cluster.

When I reached for it,
they plumed upward,
tickling everything.

Puffing past the crossed metal
shadow playing on the stage
before the glassed specimens passing
through the no-door

Leaving us on our knees peeking
through celestial
mud.

premenstrual dysphoria disorder as burning haibun – andrea lianne grabowski (she/her)

the shortest days of the year. shortest temper of the month. i turn on myself when my father swings for my wrist. he does not know what he is doing. this is because he was afraid. or something. they call it, *the dementia grip.* my mother screams at him louder than the screaming inside my belly. this is a metaphor. she cares for us in our worst iterations; i care for them in theirs. my digestion is doing fine. i want to rip all my organs out. i keep threatening to use the serrated knife but i don't want to pass out. it's just a feeling. it's the most swallowing thing in the world. just for now. i've felt like this in this house for sixteen years, once in a while. the guilt is like a gilded christmas card envelope crumpled in the recycling bin. i am guilty of nothing. i ran out of magnesium & martyrdom. i run in circles of crumpled tissues. even a breakfast sausage package can rend me to pieces. i rend myself to pieces. how to tend to my pieces? i want someone to tend to my pieces. the vitex is for the long haul & i don't have any patience. latin name over folk name. but might as well call it chasteberry. it fits, for me. even though i didn't choose that, did i? *stop playing the victim.* but i am, aren't i? of the snow & the screaming but really, of the flood of progesterone & cortisol & the way loud sounds make my brain shake & my organs twist & could i twist everyone into loving me the way i want/need/want/need if i were a demigod? my father was like hephaestus, my mother like hestia. now i'm the daughter of the god of forgetting. the daughter of a single mother. like percy. *be brave, child. hold fast.* i'm tired of redemptions.

names that sound like other names are just names. i have a beautiful orchard & i am still lonely. *ungrateful hypocrite* or, *i deserve better.* which is it? darkest days of the year. the sun sets over amidon road & my tears dried so i walked halfway up the ice. sat on zoom & talked about rurex like i pity myself, or maybe just need someone in this mitten-state who would watch my back while i climb through a broken window. *ingratiate yourself into my life, i'm begging you. do not be afraid, voice like the tides, like a mystery in a film canister.* i am always ingratiating myself only to feel like a failure or be failed or maybe just left behind. maybe it's the expectations. crumpled guilt envelope, silver & gold. let me do it right & let it work this time. but i don't know how to let go. what even is doing it right? i can't control a thing, except pathologization of my need. i bought more magnesium but i can't buy more martyrdom. wouldn't want to anyway. look at my orchard. isn't it beautiful? but aren't all the trees so far away? look at my anticipatory grief. look at my anticipatory hope. the unthinkable & the obvious. i want to rip the lights from the neighbors' fence & never run out of the house without a coat again but my organs keep twisting like i could grab a serrated knife &—well. this is the haunting of the mitten. my mother's mitten on my abandoned hand & *i'd drive you to idlewild or the abandoned concrete plant because i still don't give up hope even when i've lost the rug under my feet too many times & i don't even like cherry starbursts. do you? the great lakes we love won't be hemmed in by ice this year. it's enbridge's fault, not mine for starting to eat breakfast sausage again.*

my lips are dry & cracked & raw. i'm drunk on badger chapstick & huckleberry chapstick. i used to swing from an ironwood tree & count by tens in french before kicking my pink & orange flowered rain boots as far as they would fly. my father—hephaestus—would count in unison, fetch the rain boots. now i fetch medicine for my father—the god of forgetting. his muscles are ironwood-strong when he squeezes my fingers. so tight i wish he'd break them so i'd have no choice but to not help him anymore. no choice but for him to leave. last month i wrote that if his muscles are iron, let mine be water. i am pouring out saltwater. too numb to be anything else. there are so many wooly angels on the christmas tree. wooly angel in the window, for a moment, hanging from my fingers, waiting for this to pass.

//

days  i turn on myself ▮▮▮▮▮▮ my ▮▮▮▮ scream ▮▮

▮▮ is a metaphor. ▮ i want to ▮▮▮▮▮ threaten ▮▮▮▮ to
▮▮▮▮▮▮▮▮▮ like ▮▮▮ this house ▮▮▮ the guilt is ▮▮▮

crumpled ▮ nothing. ▮ i ▮ can rend me to
pieces. i ▮ tend to my pieces? i want someone ▮ for
the long haul ▮ patience ▮ over folk name. ▮
▮ chasteberry ▮ fits ▮ me. ▮ *stop playing* ▮
aren't i ▮ the snow & the ▮ flood of ▮ the way i
want/need/want/need ▮? my father was ▮ the god of forgetting.
▮

i'm tired of redemptions. names ▮ are just names ▮
▮ & i am still lonely. ▮ darkest ▮ f sun
sets over ▮ my tears ▮ halfway up the ice ▮
▮ like i ▮ just need someone in this mitten-state
who would ▮ *ingratiate* ▮ *into my life* ▮
▮ *like the tides* ▮ let me do it ▮ but i don't
know how ▮ pathologization of my need ▮ my
orchard. ▮ aren't all the trees so far away? look at my
▮ grief ▮ hope. the unthinkable & ▮
the lights ▮ run out of the house ▮ twisting like ▮
▮ a serrated knife ▮ this is the haunting of ▮
my mother's mitten ▮ *i'd drive you* ▮ *because*
i still don't give up ▮ *the rug* ▮ *&* ▮ *cherry*
starbursts. ▮ *the great lakes* ▮ *won't be* ▮ *it's*
enbridge's fault ▮

my lips are ▮ drunk on ▮ huckleberry ▮ & ▮ pink &
orange flowered rain boots ▮ they would fly ▮ would
count ▮ medicine for ▮ forgetting. ▮
ironwood-strong when ▮ i wish ▮ i'd have ▮ choice ▮ to
▮ let mine be water ▮ pouring out ▮. anything else. ▮
wool ▮ in the window ▮ hanging ▮, waiting
▮

//

▮ threaten ▮ guilt ▮ tend ▮ the

▮ ice. ▮ i ▮ need ▮ my ▮ grief ▮ lights ▮
i'd ▮ *drive* ▮ *i* ▮ *don't* ▮ forget ▮

Ivy/For Her - Giselle Linder (she/her)

my head is a haunted house hollowed out
and I'm tired of asking people to come home
the telephone rattles like a smoker's cough when I call
and I feel the ringing sound ground down to my bones

but when the graveyard light catches the ends of your hair
I feel for the first time in years
like more of a woman than a prayer

listen—moth wings flutter over the curve of my stomach
and over the arch of my neck

you should follow the way they fall and put your hands there

we would lose a day, perhaps a year
shedding those sordid skins of despair

but what's a year to an hour with you?
what excuse can I give for being scared?

I long to curl myself over the crest of your body
the way ivy crawls over stone

I don't know much of these lives that we lead
but I know we shouldn't have to wander through them alone

you say that I'm your favorite – Ivy L. James (she/her)
—after Reneé Rapp

and you're my favorite too—
          the one I see the most,
                    the one I think about the most too.

I'd drop an armful of mirrors
          if you crooked your finger and said *come*
                    here, I need you
          and all the bad luck would be worth it
if I could attend you for a minute.

I watch your hands tremble;
          I watch you braid your hair;
                    I watch you watch the one you want.
                              (she's not me,
                                        though we look similar
                                                  if I squint.)

I watch and I watch and I watch and I
          shatter like those mirrors, fragile but eager
                    to reflect you when our eyes meet,
          it's you you you let me *show* you—
but you glance away and I remember

I'm only her reflection.

The Nirvana Burning Brings – Matthew Feinstein (he/him)

Before the noose of apocalypse threatens our necks,

       I ask—   because I can't distinguish
                                             hostel from cottage—

is this comfort,

      love?

Is this paradise?

Blink authentic,
               if yes.

                       Speak
                               if I missed something.

You're miles
smarter than me.

Yes, education exacerbates a crisis' sting.
Yes, our choke-chained earth homes

dread inside you.

But supermarkets make great dance clubs—

            let's sub-par   Ring-Around-the-Rosie

                on this linoleum floor
                until collapse—

                bonk our silly human heads,
                laugh like

                                    pre-shame   Adam and Eve.

This can be paradise,
regardless.

The world is choking,
regardless.

Mother death will snatch us,
regardless. To think,

your eyes shone,
                              moments ago,
at the cheap décor
of a mother chimp
clutching her young.

Let her gold paint smile
remind you of generational danger.

Evolution is a nasty design—
the lion's maw still rips
the antelope's stomach,
and we wither.

Lest we forget,
               biology is a loan shark.

Our birthright *is*
               our deathright.

Yes, bombs fall
bountiful.

Yes, outside's pattering
an ungodly June phenomenon.

Yes, the climate, but you still love
the rain—

how drops land on your pineal gland
                              like wisdom
                              herself.

The Burning Nirvana Brings – Matthew Feinstein (he/him)

This attic called world,
    we do not own it.

Its limes. Its petals. The teeth
        it gifted us.

The more I ruminate on being alive
    —its beautiful miseries—

      the more language
        is culprit.

          A whodunnit where the killer breastfed
             the victim.

          Where everyone scapegoats everyone
            in the end.

The culprit birthed the velvet Chesterfield. The culprit—a
trickster—
throws atop our heads, blankets
sewn with ignorant
threads.   How could
          something so pure
             slaughter
          something so pure?

We own not the attic
but the décor we crafted
with language: Grandfather clocks, Lazy Boy
recliner with beer coaster.

Human reputations—a decapitated pilot
        whose name synonymous
                with training
                        on plane crash
                                prevention.

Human stigmatizations—a man,
            unable to afford psych meds,
                runs like a stranger
                                into traffic.

                        The human doing human wrongs
                        society deems inhuman—
                        burning cities, apathy
                        for the dead.

I've held angels as devils
in memory
            after they stranded me
                    on a frozen June night

                    because we bastardized
                            the climate, bought
                                and ate, and plenty turned
                                    scarce, and scarce turned

                                        apocalypse.

We killed boredom
to block life's
ugliness.

            We killed
            mysterious awe.

                    We killed
                    nirvana.

We, the billions, rummage the attic,
    wander the orange-glow forest
        to be readopted

    —like cookie-munching children—

                        by the void.

A Flash – LindaAnn LoSchiavo (she/her)

To hear my mother tell it, after childbirth her spine rebelled, becoming a cold and rumbling fault line. A difficult breech delivery ruined everything.

To hear my mother tell it, a respectful infant should politely slide from the womb, not unlike a love letter shrugging off its scented pink envelope. But a willful neonate deliberately positions herself awkwardly in the birth canal, taut as a bowstring emerging from its warrior cave of shadows. *En garde.*

To hear my mother tell it, from that point, good health slipped free of her, becoming a fancy hat she never could afford again. Her prenuptial decades were later mythologized into a golden era of uncomplicated serenity.

Her lies bore only a passing likeness to reality. Around me, the purifying flames of authenticity were stifled, denuding the landscape of affectionate memories, scorching everything but blame, illusions. Cherishing slipped away like days we couldn't hold onto, truth's mouth sewn shut. We never mastered the mechanics of mother-daughter camaraderie.

My devotion clicked its heels in steady, meaningless rhythm, invisible, buried under her volcanic scorn—until one day nursing was necessary. Cancer helped adorn my mother with patience, her acidic breath pausing to accept the spoon that brought breakfast, her daylight swallowing fast.

Apologies emerged, released like doves. Between us a tight-chested pause exhaled.

Perhaps she had grasped we only love so long.

Namsan Tower - Jong Yun Won (he/him)

Before I came back to the Motherland
I came back to the Motherland

garnished with my small-town spiky hair
earthy plaid, and still ugly relative to white people.

My mom's friends who said I was handsome
were liars, but they gave me manwon
to buy jjajangmyun, so I said, thanks.

After that, I went away by myself
because I was a lonely black-bean

I discovered the subway bodies—dormant noodles
wearing black sauce, without vinegar

somehow found myself on black namsan
and the sky was an empty bowl

from the tower, I saw many depressed cars
blinking bright oil over the hangang
also black, perhaps made of sauce

even now, my tongue is a traffic jam
of wok-inspired fire delaying
families during Myeongjeol.

But I'd be doing jjajangmyun a disservice
if I didn't admit I've had some time to ferment

to remember the heat that night
the cicadas, my black hair flopping around
as I ran down the mountain
as my mother once had.

In the bathtub – Eugenie Carabatsos (she/her)

midnight unscathed
by UV rays
galactic filament
under droplets
honest
free

in June, replace womanhood
with femininity
wash sand from line
between seen and un
my midnight weakened,
atone

until then, cherish
secret universe
pure self,
the brilliance
of cosmic threads

First published in Pink Panther

Shelley - J M Roberts (she/her)

because you've been traveling so long,
so far, even if just in your head
and you're exhausted, I know.
Do you think we should get a room here

while we're still sane? All work,
no play, that's the way I've always been, Jack.
Winding telegraphs around my fingers, state lines
cat's cradle, I sit hunched in your car—

that's a different kind of crazy.
You drive, building the road with your eyes—
that's your kind of crazy. Your ability
to graft reality from sheer will, but still you won't

give me a line, please, give me a line. Or pour
me a drink (you) sit me down tell (me) how
can somebody go crazy with so
much room to run? What I'm afraid of:

A pantry. What you're afraid of:
Too much time to think.

moving out – Malachy Harris (they/she)

if you leave milk in your
  fridge for more than six weeks
    it begins to divide and unpeel itself
     solid and liquid lie in layers soaked
    in each other and if you leave it for longer
  your flatmates will eventually
come home and ask you silly questions

    i am a floppy disc sometimes or sometimes
   an apple sometimes a table a garden hose
  often the growing mound of uncollected cans
waiting to be swept up in arms in some
  begrudging act of care a do you really live
    like this i am a tidy room when nobody is home
    i am the call of what's left swept under a bed

     my eyes are thick with paint
     voice artificially high i cover
     myself in glitter and hang across my
     knees i cut myself shaving and do not
     stem the blood watch myself change
     shape against the mirror

     i think i disassociate when i stare too long
           and he stares back   that man who follows
           me around   but so does everyone

when i was a girl
     i told you
        i wanted to be eve
        to take a bite
        and grip the sides
        amid tumbles of disbelief

Litany of G – Nona Lea (she/they)
 —after Franny Choi

This G began screaming for it was the G of grieving and having grieved it was G of absence G for gods who don't answer G of the gleam of emblems of authority G of birds that began with G but who no longer make sound G of a mother suckled to death G of the gleeful cackling after forest fire G of the names without graves G of a malignant growth G of which we agreed was the final litmus G of goodnight and goodbye G that gave like no other G for it was generous with gluttony G of gums lined in ghost of gold G of having and not having G trying to make sense in ghazals G of post-world revisionist gospel G of gasping G of what they call therapy for social ills G of clenched knuckles and tight smiles G that commands: be gentle G of rules enforced through ghouls G of gatekeeping information G for gods' creatures favored and systematically fucked G that doesn't stop G that begins and ends with G of ceaseless humming G of I'm tired of begging G of witnessing and witnessing and witnessing G ushering in the silence G for being told the G is not actually a G and it's justified, really G of yass #girlbossing G of chanting cultish jargon G that passes onto another G of not G devouring the other G for *some* goddamn reason

if only by a step. – Audric Adonteng (he/him)

we sunbathe in the hourglass,
as more pours over our bodies.

we build sandcastles on the seashore,
& destroy them before the tide.

we dance barefoot on acorns and twigs,
as a flurry of leaves fill the sky.

we climb the old maple-leaf oak fence,
& laugh as we remove each other's splinters.

we chase each other through mud in our sunday best,
& know what it means to live.

we take steps and don't know where we will land,
because we know we will land.

Sink or Swim – Travis Stephens (he/him)

My favorite brother tossed me into the river.
He was strong & laughing & I was small
so I flew a long way
to cold water
                    sputter
                            flail splash
panic.

That's it, he said, waist deep out of reach,
That's how you learn to swim.
Current dragged at my legs.
We were skinny kids & didn't float.
We got hit & sometimes deserved it.

Look, he wasn't always my favorite brother
& he had a practiced eye for
quick, hurtful remarks followed with a laugh.
Just kidding.

Egrets walk the shore of a marsh, watching
for shapeless bits trying to swim.
Tadpoles taste of copper & fertilizer & fish
left out in the sun.
Eventually this brown water will be drawn in motion,
a stream that becomes a river that tries
to drown farm kids, those shivering gasping
snot-nosed boys who all look the same.

To teach me to drive my favorite brother
let me steer the pickup through the field
as he tossed steel T-posts off the back.
I could barely reavch the pedals.
We were dividing the hayfield in half
to let the cattle graze the rest.

When the pickup front tires lurched into a ditch
I stomped the gas & Physics Lessons emerged,
Motion and Equal Opposites.
My brother was tossed from the pickup bed,
landing badly & rising. Furious.

Good fences make good neighbors
but thick walls & distance are preferable.
Listen, don't believe everything I tell you;
you weren't there.
All my brothers were my favorite & my sister too.
I was the one drowning while everyone
          watched.

Groundhog Day - Georgie Contreras (she/her)

The more things change, the more they stay the same:
I started laughing before Ant even finished the cliché
But he knew how to get underneath my skin
It seemed to be the only thing he was good for
A balmy summer night on an Allston porch
I had waited until he was properly wasted
To tell him about you, how we met
He then asked to see a picture, only to say:
Your ex has the better smile

I haven't been writing much these days
Unless you count the Notes section of my cry log
Your name and a sentence or two, over and over
I started keeping a journal in the fall of 2016
Sometimes it was hard to maintain when—

        I've written this poem before
Questions I don't ask and the answers I won't receive
You could have mistaken me for a child with an imaginary friend
The conversations I wrote between me and Ant, after he left

What does it feel like? Like something else
This script I was given the summer I turned 19
I take it out sometimes to reread and mark up
I'll grab my favorite pink gel pen and try to ignore
How much of a coward you are, how pathetic
I am for trying to forget
The ending never changes

Funny - Allison Thung (she/her)

how politely we speak to each other now, as though that entire lifetime took place only in our imaginations. Exchanges so delicate, like we feared the words would break as we uttered them, as if we never broke promises, broke into laughter at inapt moments, broke wind, broke up, made up, broke up again. As if some part of us doesn't still sit in that hotel lobby on that Friday night become Saturday morning, hands sweaty from keeping a hold on our laptop bags so they didn't slide over the edge of that too-small couch, pondering all the im/possibilities we w/could n/ever pursue. Or in those cable cars on which you kept insisting despite your fear of heights, gazing out at a view I forgot existed and maybe never truly appreciated when I remembered. Or in the living room of your house watching television with your parents after dinner, my dread at returning to my own life only growing. But anyway, *I'm fine, thank you. How are you doing?*

yes, we always travel in multiple – tommy wyatt (he/they)

falling asleep at youth group
because we extended energy
shifting into translucent light
as we hide in the basement,
sifting ourselves to shadow
and dust, an airtight stillness,
skilled camouflage, can't say
we're not shy of trauma when
we seek a constant state
of realm-altering realness
as a game of jailbreak.

*

exorcising memories of playing 2006's version of *Call of Duty* with
a boy who rode our bus, for one day only; simulated violence only
okay'd by our parents through verbal warfare, or *The Sims* where
we'd roleplay Mom and Dad who keep losing the bassinet (not
baby, see object) to a social worker, a *Bustin' Out* glitch that felt
realitytrue when a doctor knew we were malnourished and
jaundiced to our parents' approval and how she asked if we were
okay in private, if we were safe.

*

dreaming we're at WestArts instead,
writing lyrics that liken us to demons,
baited by body, to say we pray to prey

on us in the same skinsuit? how we
look to dice flesh if it means there's
less to pick at, if it means

how we speak in accidental

edgelord pandering:
ghoul seeking vessel

kind of shit, and i know why
we lunged to cast ourselves out
in after school special style

with summer draining
us loose and fevered: we want
to be seen or destroyed.

The Gods of All Knowledge - Marc Meierkort (he/him)

They say evidence lies in black holes.
They say wormholes go back in time.

They say time is stacked like pancakes.
They say dark matter is soupy like syrup.

They say Heaven is a Place on Earth.
They say Heaven is in Your Mind.

They say Heaven is a Stairway.
They say the Bar is called Heaven.

They say God is a volcano god.
They say the Pope is infallible.

They say charity begins in Rome.
They say the Church is cash-poor.

They say priests bleed them dry.
They say orthodox damn straight.

They say on day six comes sex.
They say woman comes next.

in their own time - Linda M. Crate (she/her)

maybe you'll find me
in the forest,
leaning against the
kindness of trees or dancing
in the laughing creeks
of living water;

maybe you'll see me caught
in the spellwork of sunlight
whispering through the trees—

because i know this is the way
i was meant to journey,

following the wild thistles and thorns
of my heart and allowing the roses
to bloom in their own time.

midnight mystery – Yuu Ikeda (she/they)

you smells like midnight.
you smells like 0:00 a.m.

you cocoon everything,
you swallow everything,
you make everything naught.

you wear the moonlight as a ring of diamond.
your cheeks with tears blinking
are like a silky scarf.

you put on perfume named 'midnight'.

you are wrapped in mystery of
midnight that fascinates me, overwhelming

Driving to the Beach you Fantasized Visiting – Matthew Feinstein
(he/him)

My dashboard thrones the photo of you
aiming a slingshot at Central Valley Sun.
I replay, in my head, two months
prior to your death.
High school graduation:
You, pale boy in the wheelchair—
lopsided atop your bald head,
your grad cap.
pale   pale   pale   pale
through my mind as
you spoke hope.
A congregation of heat
in cheap metal seats
burned us all ceremony—
all summer, we burned.
The endemic stalking
of life's minute hand.
When you died, *Cancer*
by My Chemical Romance blared
while your ex, in my backseat,
squealed *why* toward stars
like a sow above her
bolt-pistoled mother.
At your funeral, I was lost
in your casket—embalmed doll
of you so foreign—like sub-par
biology...which, I suppose,
synonymous with cancer.
Tonight, sand will chalk
my inner toes when I reach
the shore—night's dark blue
circling me and my gooseflesh
will rise like a prophet,

and how gorgeous the scene—
like the universe knew cinema,
and I'll wonder if you marrionetted
the breeze...which I suppose
synonymous with *I'm here.*
Your favorite root beer
in my hand—not to drink
but pour.

heart – Michelle Young (she/her)

mother plagued
with dreams of daughter's corpse
glassy eyes / dry mouth / cold flesh
she tells you
do not allow
anyone
into your heart

words pound deeper into skull
hammer hits nails
nails dig deeper
bone cracks—
destroys all logic

hair cut short because it's harder to pull
avoid touch because you remember bruises
leave the house with sweaty palms
burn work schedules

breathe

heart threatens to crawl up throat
beating violently
cough it up
spit it out

Brain Fried Like Popcorn - Madeline Rosales (she/her)

I paged Dr. Timothy Leary and he said to fry my brain,
so by twenty-one, I was running on bare-bone fumes.
Leary prompted, "Why not?" But I called the Angels
to forward me to God, and He said, "Don't do that if it hurts."
I haven't been sober since.
But those off-white popcorn ceilings still haven't quit
fracking and pricking my vision, usually clouded by illusions
and hallucinations, scratching themselves like sloppy doodles
and Rembrandt nocturnes into my head. Though critics scoff,
I'm drawn to their chaotic simplicity, and their endlessly monotone
personalities. Damn. They make me feel this itch to purge
my nothing-feeling. How do you express "nothing"?
But how do I ignore this holy sadness that is *not* like what King Saul
felt upon his own sword, but just the steady buzz
of radio static echoing the emptiness of a popcorn ceiling?
I wonder everyday if it's just depression or the aftermath of DMT
throwing me to the curb and demanding I confront the victims
it left behind. As I gaze up at the ceiling, a memory floods me.
And I'm back at my old man's office building.
I'd punch in for some data entry gig now
and then to cover my dry account. It was warmer in the floor below
his, and always they was piping elevator "muzak."
I knew every tune, even though I was never supposed to sing along.
And I remember every beat resonating with me, because we
both were just a form of intentional meaninglessness. In another
story, we are sold for twenty or 30 pieces of silver by brothers
or disciples. And love leads us into a white and soulless place,
because it was a kiss that killed Jesus before the cross was ever built.

Because there are snakes in the grass of the lawns we watered.
Because I have fucked on the grounds of every temple, and I have
spilt blood upon their pews. Because I dreamed of divinity.
But what am I doing, staring up at rental-friendly, off-white
ceilings, and reminiscing on white-noise "muzak" when
Dr. Leary has been on the line for fifteen years? I've spent fifteen
years trying to make room in my skull for anything else but
acid and popcorn.

our pot runneth over: – Audric Adonteng (he/him)

waakye leaves loiter in lukewarm water
tears dry into salt deposits across my brown face
dirt and grass stains form an x on my denim overalls,
time will pass over this body.
prune juice trickles onto my forehead.
tap, tap, tap.
our eyes do not shift.
soft footsteps cross the roof, and the white settles on my home.
tap, tap, tap
the trees are gone and the world is dead, i say.

why did we rake the children from the trees and make piles of
their bodies?
& play as the warm colors filled the air?
why did the world halt and give silence an indefinite revival?

but my mother tells me the leaves will return.
waakye leaves begin to steam.
the water attempts to escape the pot.
i look into her eyes // i don't believe her.

for my mother's eyes are brown. her skin is brown.
the skin of trees, the brief chestnut flash through the lawn,
the hollow husk bridging both sides of the river,
the maple oak fence, the splinters in my knee.
the leaves (briefly)

so my mother must be a leaf.
when do you turn back green, i ask.
she laughs // i do not believe her

my curiosity is overwhelmed by grief.

she holds me // the tears escape faster

the waakye leaves are screaming.
the pot runneth over.
she holds me.

the air in the kitchen is smoke.
there is no air between us.

In Stillness – Liam Chimba (he/him)

She was having a right bubble bath about it,
Incensed, apoplectic, all from the gut,
The kind with crow's feet next to her eyes,
She kept laughing and
I swallowed needles in my coffee.

She says it's because I'm pretty,
Boys are gonna want that,
Want me, like it's my fault,
Like it's funny that it happened.

I never managed to finish the story,
What happened in the bathroom,
A sickly smell of cinnamon,
The flickering Yankee candle,
The shame that I could never wash off.

She said something, I deferred,
It all circled back to that candle,
Watching my shadow cast out onto the tiles,
So clean, so pure,
Until I moved and turned it black.

I wanted to keep my faith,
To watch the light shimmer against my face,
But each movement threatened to blow it out,
And I learnt how to hold my breath.

In perfect stillness, I watched her laugh.

Original Sin - Krystle Eilen (she/her)

mind like a relic akin

to a serpent;

the boa snags tight

the arm of the flailing

child;

perhaps to wince

is pressure enough

to absent the swollen eye,

for to look into mind

bright

would be to struggle

the plight.

Diary of a Lotus Eater – Caitlin Annette Johnson (she/they)

Lick it again and feel
the soft pearl of oblivion.
It's not dark like you'd think.
There is light. The gleeful
dapple of mirror balls.
The undiluted sunshine
of a mind less burdened,
laid bare to pure pleasure.
There must be light there—
otherwise, why go headfirst
every morning, right away?
I ate the fruit because
I needed to be easier to love.
I ate the fruit because
I needed to be softer, milder,
less lashed by a merciless god.
I needed a tongue of white lace,
perhaps a palm of real laughter—
I needed to drink and touch
back all the gods that loved me.

Fragile Paradise – Matthew Feinstein (he/him)

We drag you like trash down sunbaked driveways.
Your fire glows like a child
begging for cookies at midnight.
Your righteous smoke tantrum choke-chains
movie theaters, citizens, streetlamps. When I visit
your ruins, hold me in your blackened branches.
Goodbye, holy spit of God. Hello, Lucifer's
cooking pot. Boil us like livestock.
We'll curse false gods like victims
when firefighters pull from the rubble
a charred child clutching a cookie.

how to put ten minutes of anxiety into Google Maps – Ivy L. James
(she/her)

Start at the house you grew up in, the walls cracked and thin like rice paper, the locks untrustworthy. Ease your way down the driveway. Don't think too hard about where you're going. Don't think too hard about whether you want to be there.

Head southeast on the silent road, the road you learned to look both ways on even though no one was ever coming. It was safe, or it should've been.

305 ft

Turn left toward shame. Toward the eyes that track your every move, waiting for you to reach for something they've declared off-limits. Toward the taloned claws that curl, waiting, waiting, waiting.

0.5 mi

Turn left to the life you used to live. The life you preached to anyone who would listen. The life you were so sure was the right path for you, for everyone. It was easier to grab on to that anchor than admit something was deeply wrong with it all.

0.3 mi

Continue straight on; don't make any jokes about how this is the straightest thing about you. Ignore the vice around your throat that matches your two fists around the steering wheel. Don't choke as you pass the gas station, the Goodwill, the abandoned farm. This was always the route you took. You used to love the drive. You could love it again if you tried.

0.2 mi

Continue onto the straight and narrow. Continue. *Continue.* No, you're doing it wrong.

3.6 mi

At the traffic circle that used to be a four-way stop, take the first exit onto the road the church is named after. The word on the signpost burns your eyes. Your vision goes blurry. Your cheeks are wet. It's not the signpost.

2.0 mi

Turn right into the parking lot. Don't breathe too fast and shallow. Don't talk too loud. Don't hide your wedding ring, but also don't draw attention to that hand in case someone thinks you're showing off your life of sin. Don't cry when the pastor digresses about homosexuality and purity and conditional love. Don't think too hard about how intensely you used to believe all this. Don't think too hard. Don't think. Don't be.

Your destination is on the left.

FICTION

Witness - Amita Basu (she/her)

The news networks had become a tangle of rumours, conspiracy theories, and deepfakes impossible to tell from reality. Our pendulum swung from skepticism to panic and we wondered whether we'd waited too long. We awoke the children in the dead of night. Down the street, the gas-masked vigilantes hammered on doors, smashed through windows, and dragged those suspected of harbouring the plague out into the street. They opened the firehose and held their victims in place, fire-retardant gloves clutching fistfuls of singeing hair. Deep into the children's ears we drove silicone earplugs. These screams were not theirs to witness.

He still had his badge, so nobody stopped him as he drove the speeding school bus full of our children out the city. I stayed back with our goats and turkeys, squirrels and dogs. Lamed and blinded, abused and abandoned, the animals in our sanctuary had kept their hearts and had helped our orphans find theirs again. Maybe in the morning I could load them all into the truck.

I awoke to find the coops torn up, the kennels smashed to matchsticks, and the door to the pen swinging on its hinges. I felt guilty for feeling grateful that they'd been taken away before they were killed, that I hadn't had to bear witness.

Then the news channels united to flash one image: the bomb, which we'd been waiting for, had dropped at last. In a way, I thought, when I could think again, it was a relief. It was over. Now surely, like in the movies, like in history, the nations would unite to sign a new peace treaty. Then I saw where the bomb had fallen: on the city to which he was driving our children.

I jumped into our sedan with its hacking-cough engine and jammed-shut backdoors and sped down the interstate, up the mountainside. On the mountain pass I saw our school bus. I jumped out of the car with streaming eyes. Thank God: they'd stopped just outside the ten-mile blast radius. They must've abandoned the bus and left a note telling me which way to walk.

A chill fell over me. My feet began to drag. Heart racing, eyes lowered from the windows, I climbed into the bus. The engine was still on, groaning amiably. The spring air, sun-warmed, kissed my neck as it ran in the door.

Facing the city he'd been driving towards, the city that had become ashes, he sat. The wrinkles in his skin had become the grooves in bark. His toes, sheathed in wood, grew down through the bus floor branching into intricate roots. His arms—reaching towards the city, pointing, raised upwards to God, beseeching— were almond branches flowering white-and-pink through the roof-hatch.

Wood, too, were all our children. Their mouths were sealed in bark. Their butts, jumping off their seats at the moment of impact, were rounded humps in tree trunks. Their pointing fingers sprouted tender green. Only their eyes were still human, open and lidless, frozen from the horror of bearing witness.

Wild goose – Dean Hel (they/them)

The ceremony is set to begin at the first light of dawn. Mary stands rooted to the ground, not sitting. The others are late.

Through the clearing, the moon hides in her veils. Mary feels its slow descent inside her spine. Agitated wind slaps hair into her face. Icy drops from the earlier rain fall from the canopy like needles into her exposed skin. She refuses to shift. Her knees lock in place. Her eyes dilate from lack of use. Her teeth gnaw at a bit of tongue though; she needs something.

A rustle, too loud for a nocturnal animal, breaks her paralysis: her back pulls up, her bare feet temper the ground. Mary does not say, where have you been.

Eleanor leads, then Justine, Kat. Mary does not ask, where is she.

"Get in position," says Eleanor, as if it matters now. Kat is still wearing a gold necklace and earrings, the fool.

Mary does not say, fool.

They form a useless circle with a person-shaped gap. Mary feels the last remnant of thin moonlight slide from her bare skin and clenches her stomach against the thing that threatens to rise in her throat.

"She's coming," Eleanor lies.

Justine finally sheds her blouse and stands. Eleanor hisses. Justine turns her back, drops her cotton panties, turns back, a hand above her pubis. Mary does not say, fool.

They shift, stalks in the wind. A bluejay whistles a note. Mary closes her eyes, prays a litany, swallows a bit of her mangled tongue. The gods accept her humble sacrifice: Gilian appears in the circle, breathless, too loud, her features all wrong, filling the air with the acrid scent of sweat.

For a moment Mary is seized by the temptation to unlock her knees and break the circle, break *them*, pull at their useless hair and limbs like so many cotton-padded dolls.

Then she takes Gillian's hand, she closes the circle, she frees all the air trapped inside her lungs. She tilts the column of her neck and the pale blue light of dawn paints it like silk.

The women let go of Mary's hands as they rise into the air.

Mary does not say, what about me?

Soon, the sky swallows them entire, even the vain, even the foolish.

Mary stands rooted to the ground. Shards of sunlight crown her.

Starlings – Sarah Blackshaw (she/her)

By the time the adults across the globe noticed what was happening, it was almost too late. I don't know why we didn't spot it sooner, to be honest—although of course I do know, I'd just prefer not to admit that we were too wrapped up in our own lives to realise that our children were struggling. That our children were dying.

We noticed some things, as individual households or communities sometimes do, thinking that their difficulties are unique. The pervasive nihilism that had taken hold at the turn of the century, as climate change and poverty and two more world wars took their toll. The dangerous games being played online, daring children to risk life and limb, and the small clusters of teenagers that died together in different flavours of incident marked emphatically by the news cycle as "accidents." By the time we realised that they weren't accidents, that they were coordinated, we just were not prepared to cope. We didn't realise that it was the end of the world as we knew it.

The government did all the usual things that people ten years behind a curve normally do. They banned the sale of bleach to those under 25, put a curfew and internet restrictions on all teenagers, even introduced some brief prison sentences for people who tried and failed to harm themselves—but the kids were *really* trying by that point, and succeeding, and the government had no choice but to watch on in horror as our population of under 18s became smaller and smaller. And secretly, I don't blame them. Why would they want to live in a world like this one? Faced with the choice, they simply opted out.

It was clear that nothing the government could do would help, and nothing we could do as individuals was helping either. I sat at night, watching my daughter sleep, knowing that tonight her chest rose and fell with the evenness of her breathing but that tomorrow this wasn't guaranteed in the way I thought it had been. Saffie had explained the issues to me in snatches, in whispered acknowledgment that she didn't want to live in a world where she would starve or burn in 30 years anyway, but I mistook that for the anxiety of youth and ignored her until a failed overdose of my antidepressants made me sit up and take notice. She was one of the lucky ones, as four of her friends had already made their way across the dividing line that none of us thought our children would want to cross. Now I wonder if she was truly lucky, if she had any idea of what was coming next.

The first scientist to manage it called it transubstantiation, which pissed off about three of the world's major religions in one go, but as they had little power at that point nobody really cared. The premise was so simple, and so bizarre, that people couldn't quite believe it at first. Then the studies were published and people saw how well it worked, and there was no stopping them after that.

Imagine a way to reduce the population of humans so that we were using up less resources, whilst simultaneously increasing the animal population to help restore the earth's natural balance. That was transubstantiation in a nutshell, although the actual how of it is lost on me. All I know is that any human who felt that they didn't want to live as a human anymore, who felt the weight of climate change and fear, could go to a facility outside Cambridge and undergo a procedure that would turn them into an animal. Well, initially the plan was to turn people into endangered species, but as time went on the scientists realised that the process only really worked to do one thing. So now, there was a choice better than death: human or bird.

Saffie jumped at the idea almost immediately, of course. I wanted more information, some assurance that it was safe, but the information available to us was instantly clouded by people with an agenda, as it often is. The government thought it was a wonderful idea and a way to restore the populations of our struggling forests, to give us jays and wrens and nuthatches back in areas where they had gone almost extinct. The usual suspects, distrustful of the government and science, were convinced that it was some kind of plot to murder us without it being obvious—it was less distressing to believe that your loved one had become a bird than to believe that they had died by suicide, and it solved our overpopulation problem virtually overnight. Some people claimed to have read the studies, noting that the viability of the procedure was only 40%, but the fact that there were no half-bird, half-human creatures wandering around put paid to their anxieties. Of course, if you define viability as "does this kill you or not," then suddenly you have a different question to answer. But Saffie was excited, and I was sceptical but also just so pleased to see her happy again, so bright and calm and clear in purpose. How could I not want her to be happy?

I wasn't allowed to go with her—that was in the conditions of the contract she signed, hundreds of pages long in size 10 font. She could not choose the type of bird she wanted to be (that was up to her DNA and the way the transubstantiation process interacted with her), she could not have visitors at the facility before or after the procedure, she could not talk to anyone outside of immediate family about signing the contract. She would just disappear, and her friends would have to hope that she had become the Saffie that she wanted to be, free and full of flight.

Ten days after she left, a starling showed up at my window. We get starlings a lot around here, but this one seemed different, tapping at the glass with its shiny beak and staring at me through deep, dark eyes. I remember that it was sunny that day, an incongruously bright warm day in February, and the starling's feathers shone dark blue, soft purple, forest green, all of Saffie's favourite colours. There was no doubt in my mind that this was my daughter, back from the facility and forever changed.

There is only one rule for the loved ones left behind. If you see a bird that you think is your transubstantiated child, you have to leave it alone. No enticing with food, no touching, and certainly no keeping as a pet. These are wild animals now, not your wayward daughter come home tamed. As I looked at the Saffie-starling, I missed her desperately. I don't suppose that I had been the best mother overall, too clingy and cloying, too interested in what was going on in her mind. She never let me in. Well, I resolved, now she would have no choice.

Over the next week, the starling kept coming back—as did others, due to the number of mealworms I was spreading through my tiny garden, but I knew which one was my Saffie. As she became more accustomed to me, she became bolder, and then it was only a matter of putting some mealworms in a cage and letting her get comfortable before gently sliding the clasp over the door.

She fought me, of course, her tiny body thrashing against the glass and metal. I spoke to her in soothing tones, darling Saffie, my Saffie, and I told her how I was going to keep her safe, how I'd failed her so badly when she had been human. No child should want to die. No parent should ignore that cry of desperation, and now all we had was her starling life, starting fresh. We had our disagreements, even in this form: she bit me once when I was giving her fresh water and I was so shocked that she went without dinner for two days as punishment. Just like when she was human. Eventually, she learned to stop fighting, becoming used to her glass room, although I know the other starlings in the garden kept away once they realised what I'd done. She only had me for company, and I only had her.

We stayed like this for a while, Saffie-starling and me. I never let her out—truth be told, I was too scared that she would fly away and never come back, the way she had when she had left for the facility. I'd begged her to stay, and she just shook her head and went anyway. Some days the memory of this angered me, and she would get no food or water. Some days I was full of remorse and would brush her feathers and sing to her, but to do this I had to wrap her in a towel so that she didn't try to bite me. Peck me, I suppose the term would be. I would unwrap her piece by piece to brush her tiny little wings, her beautiful head, her elegant neck. But I knew it wouldn't last, that it was a temporary happiness. She was getting more restless, throwing her soft body against her cage on a more regular basis.

Two years later, they came to me on another bright February day to tell me that she was dead. Due to a change in government, more scrutiny was being applied to the transubstantiation process, and a new law had been passed to offer insight for those left behind. As part of this law, parents had to be told whether their child had been turned into a bird, although not which type, or if they had never made it through the process. Saffie died two hours after they gave her the first injection. She was buried near the facility, and I could go visit her if I wanted. I didn't want to. I cried for ten hours after they left, and if I think too much about her, I know that I will never stop.

I released the starling that night. It hopped out of the cage, looking warily at me like it suspected trickery, then took off into the woods and never looked back. And why would it? It wasn't mine to start with— but then again, neither was Saffie.

I lie awake at night now, wondering whose child I had caged and kept as my own. I hope their mother will forgive me, in time. I hope I will forgive myself, in time. When I do finally sleep I dream of wings in the darkness, flashes of blue, green, purple, strangled birdsong and the promise of flight.

Mirrors - Katrin Hessa (she/her)

She no longer remembers her name. She couldn't tell you even if you asked her.

Ro is the only name she remembers. *Ro, Ro, Ro,* she whispers in the mornings when he brushes her hair from her face and smiles tiredly and tells her get up—it's a bright morning and we have so many things to do. *Ro, Ro, Ro,* she chants it every night like a prayer while he pumps away inside her, his heavy pants prickly, warm, tight over her neck like the ghost of a stranglehold. *Ro, Ro, Ro,* she cries when she is lost in the house and momentarily forgets where she is. It never takes him very long, and he always comes for her, taking her arm; his hold tight, his face pale.

She only ever sees him.

And herself.

The mirrors are her favourite things in the house. She likes to look into the bathroom mirror, likes to trace the creases in the corners of her bruised eyes, the spots forming over her thin cheekbones. They are proof of years she doesn't remember. When she lets her eyes wander downwards, she sees her neck rimmed with red, marks she doesn't remember how she earned. She spends so much time like that—tracing whatever she can see of herself—that Ro has to beg her to please come out of the bathroom because, again, we have so many things to do today; we can't dally.

It's usually a lie. They don't do much on their days. That much she knows. He eats and he showers her and he vanishes into the office he won't let her enter.

It doesn't matter to her. The mirrors are what she cares about.

When seated at the dressing table, she likes to see the burnished brown of her hair shot through with silver. She likes to take a lock of her hair and guide it close to the mirror and try to understand why Ro likes to touch it. It is beautiful, she likes to think, though dry and prickly, and sometimes it is matted with blood. She doesn't know why and Ro only looks away when she asks him.

Sometimes she sees ghosts in the mirror. She stares at herself and thinks, for a moment, that there was somebody else who had hair like hers. Somebody else who she used to sit with at a dressing table and comb hair that looked so much like hers.

Is it a memory? A wish? A dream? She doesn't know.

There are mirrors in the hallway too. And mirrors in the living room. Mirrors in the kitchen. When she walks past any of them, her pace slows. Just to check if she is real, to check if she is herself, to check if she herself is a lie. The mirrors know her better than herself.

Mirror, mirror on the wall who remembers them all.

A touch to her shoulder draws her to the present. She blinks and turns slowly. Her muscles are stiff, so she always has to move sluggishly. Ro is looking down at her, his body covered from neck to toe. His face is strangely grave. She wants to tell him to stop looking at her like that, or she will soothe away the deep frown between his brows herself. He keeps looking at her with that frown and she doesn't like it. It makes her feel as if she's done something wrong. She likes to do things right.

"Qisma, are you alright?"

She blinks again. The air shifts. It's a little colder now, and the air feels thicker in her nose, just a little.

"Is that—my name?" she asks, her speech halting. It is always a little difficult to speak. There is a constant tightness in her throat. "Why am I—here?" She looks around. She has wandered to the front door. It's wooden and painted black. The shoe cabinet is crouched down low at her feet. The curtains on the windows are drawn shut. She doesn't know if it's day or night.

What does the world look like outside? Is there a sun? Is there a moon? She doesn't remember what they look like, though she knows they should be there. One for the day and one for the night.

"It's almost lunchtime," Ro tells her. "You wandered out of the bedroom."

She doesn't remember that.

"Come and eat with me."

Disinterested, she looks back at the door. She is filled with a sudden, overwhelming urge to step outside. She reaches out to touch the doorknob, but Ro's gloved hand takes hers before her fingers make any contact. He is quicker than she anticipates. He always is.

"It's dangerous outside."

He always says that. Of course, she doesn't remember him telling her such things, but she knows, somehow, that she is Not Supposed To Go Outside, so surely he has repeated it to her many a time. "Why?"

"You always ask that," he responds, and doesn't elaborate.

She doesn't remember asking him, though it makes sense. It is not logical to accept a rule without an explanation. It does not sit well with her to be chained. How would she eat?

Chained. At the thought, she looks down at her wrists. They are riddled with thick red marks just like the ones on her neck, ropey and tinged purple.

"Was I—chained?"

A pause. Then, "Yes."

Distrust is a bitter taste at the back of her tongue. It is a thick instinct coiling her muscles and making her step back, once, twice, thrice. Ro's eyes watch her go, dull and weary, like this is a game they have played many, many, many times.

She doesn't remember.

"Who?"

He purses his lips.

"Was it—you?" she pushes.

"It was me," he admits. He still looks grave.

Stop looking at me like that, she wants to say. *Don't you love me? That's what you told me last night. You tell me that all the time. You tell me you love me and you're sorry and you can't let me go. I never understand what you mean. You cry but you never tell me. I hate that.*

He lifts one gloved hand. His sleeves are long, covering his arms. There is a gleam of silver as he undoes the cufflinks holding his sleeves taut at the wrists. A loud clatter sounds as the metallic things fall to the floor, and she startles. She doesn't like loud things. She doesn't remember why she doesn't like loud things.

He pulls his sleeve back, revealing pale skin, shrouded with a thick dusting of dark hairs. That catches her attention. She wants to touch. She steps closer, and he stiffens, his stare wary. So she doesn't touch, though she yearns to.

He tilts his arm, and she sees multitudinous, deep marks at his wrists, his arms, red and raw. Recent. He lets her peer closer, and she sees that the marks are edged with crusted blood, assembled to form rounded shapes. Her mouth calls to those bites. She wants to rip into them and tear them anew. He must feed her.

"You bit me," he says. "You're always hungry. I have to kill to feed you. I killed a man and fed him to you last night."

She's not really paying attention. She wants to know if she bit him anywhere else. She reaches out to touch him. Hastily, he scrambles away, covering the marks with his sleeve and buttoning them up at his wrist.

She follows him.

He doesn't look at her as he backs away. "I am selfish. So selfish." His shoulders are hunched. She follows the slope of his back greedily. It is thick with muscle and flesh. It leads down to the dip of his spine where it would be so easy to rip apart. "I made you stay in this world. I can't say goodbye. I can't let you go. You're not real."

That jolts her from her distraction. How could he say that? She is real. She can feel the touch of her bare feet against the floor. She can hear him speak. She can talk. She feels it when he presses her legs open and seeks his pleasure every night. How could she not be real?

Gibberish is all he speaks.

Desperate, she dashes past him as fast as she can. She must have answers. He doesn't stop her as she finds her way down the corridor of their house, finding the place he guided her away from this morning. The doorknob opens under the pressure she exerts, twisting it to her will, and she bursts inside.

There are shelves framing the walls, a large desk at the centre of the floor. But more pressing is a window, the only uncurtained window in the house, the one window Ro has never let her see: it is a wide huge window encompassing the top half of one entire wall. It reveals pale sands, blue seas expanding till forever. For a moment, she stares, approaching.

A large, round device sits on top of Ro's desk, juts of little buttons extending outward from its body. She presses her fingers blindly over them all and the device splutters to life.

The police are still on the hunt for Qisma Ahmed, the forty-year-old Chief Inspector of homicide, whose husband was convicted of the murder of ten government officials. Ahmed was last seen alive at London's High Court of Justice, at the sentencing of her own husband, who set off a bomb attack, after which he carried her unconscious body out. Ahmed's daughter claims to have a lead, that she knows her mother is dead, that her father is defiling the body—

Slow and steady, she raises her head to look over the desk. At the corner of the room, thick silver chains gleam from the floor.

**First published by PULP Mag*

Unearthed - Annabelle Guihan Larsen (she/her)

The garage was the dark storage place for Dad's work stuff: tumbled paint cans, thick cloths splattered with a galaxy of colors; ladders and caked brushes. My paternal grandfather, Papa, was living with us in our house on Maple, when one day, he came across a mail-order ad in the back pages of the *Trib*:

Supplement Your Present Income Raising Chinchillas!

"See this?" he said to me, pointing to the ad, "Says they need more people who want to be chinchilla ranchers. A rancher, whatta ya think? And I can get your mama a fur coat out of it."

This was a time when all manner of oddities were for sale beyond the realm of commonplace and sense. Paint work was not an everyday occurrence, money was precious, and chasing curiosity seemed an easier way to pass through hard Chicago winters.

The woman in the ad had a fur cape on and was smiling. The caption underneath read: **Most ladies cannot afford such luxury. To a limited few, to own a chinchilla coat can truly be a status symbol**.

At the bottom was a photo of a little chinchilla, which looked to me like a roly-poly mouse with a long, fluffy tail. Papa's swimming pool-blue eyes widened with possibilities. The pages of the newspaper trembled between his fingers.

"Says here they don't smell and don't make much noise."

An important addition because Dad and Papa were alike in that they were stone quiet, for the most part. The difference was when Dad drank; he had a booming voice I cowered under, and phones were ripped from the wall. Ma came away with bruises which, over time, yellowed and greened on her pale skin.

My parents could last days without saying a word to one another; instead, they spoke through me: *Ask your father what he wants for dinner. Tell your mother I'm not hungry.* If I hiccupped, Dad shouted at me to leave the room.

Papa tore out the ad, which sat on the kitchen countertop, mooned with coffee stains.

Then, once the maple trees helicoptered their papery wings along the air, crates appeared. Papa took me into the garage for the unveiling. Black as pitch from wall to wall. Turpentine and old paint buckets filled with water laced the garage corners smelling of pine trees and licorice. He had stacked little metal cages on a wooden bench, chirps and squeaks came from underneath an oilcloth. In a magician's flurry, off came the cloth. Black eyes glinted down at me. They were tiny, silver-velvet looking things, and skittish as they bounced off the cage bars.

"Can I hold one?"

"No, they'll bite ya. They have big teeth."

"Will they be okay in here?"

"Sure. They're the hardy sort."

When Papa wasn't looking, through the bars, my fingers felt their buttercup fur.

I didn't know what work it entailed to be a chinchilla rancher, but I thought it was a good job. I had my pink cowboy hat I wore every day to the garage as part of my uniform. Papa fed them grass and seeds, and I helped by catching grasshoppers.

Problems started when they multiplied and their sounds became loud barks. They were in danger of Dad hearing them.

Once the weather turned warm, our maples grew purplish green, and things went south. Ma complained about the chinchilla smell leaking from the garage into her kitchen. I decided they needed a bath, so I sprayed them with water.

Days after, they lost their fur, became listless, and no longer peered out from behind the bars, instead, they huddled in the corners. Papa found out they didn't need baths; water was bad for them. They were supposed to have blue sparkle dust baths, made up of volcanic ash.

They died because of me.

I was a murderer, but if I had known about the dust bath, I would have been happy to supply it, if not just for the name alone. I imagined if they were under the eye of a better ranch hand, their pudgy bodies would whirligig in blue sparkles that filled the air with puffs of dust, instead of what turned out to be their demise.

The rotten smell enveloped the house to such a degree it was hard to breathe without feeling the must stick in my throat. I cried as their decayed bodies became buggy. Papa was too sad to throw them out. We wouldn't have any extra income like the ad had said. Ma wouldn't get her fur coat. The stink lasted forever.

We made a funeral march to the backyard and buried them in the ground underneath the maple whose new branches turned to whips from summer scorch.

Ma wiped her angry red hands down along her housecoat while she watched us.

I stood unseen in the garage doorway, the yellowed hue of the fluorescents caught onto Ma's bobby pins as she started to collapse the cages. And this was when I witnessed Papa kiss the back of Ma's wrist and say he was sorry. In a tender way, he had kissed her, soft as chinchilla's fur. He must have been sorry for the dead chinchillas that stunk the house up and sought to make up for all the luxury she wouldn't be afforded. But then, of course, I knew Papa and Ma were quiet together, in their own way.

Shortly after, in the sure of the night, Dad's drunken rampage sounded up through the floorboards in a thunderous bang.

Later then, there was another smell from the garage. Papa and Ma didn't seem to believe me when I told them about the fire.

They remained quietly playing cards while flames licked from underneath the garage door all purple and blue until the fire trucks came.

Dad's garage was never rebuilt. He came back to us as a stranger in a box of dust.

Ma and Papa made considered steps to the backyard with the box held outstretched like a serving platter. A hole was dug right next to the chinchillas. Once the box emptied, a plume of dust rose up from the ground as Ma and Papa danced slow in shades of blue.

The Healer - Leslie Cooles (she/her)

Fists hammered on the oak boards, once, twice. Exploding the latch. A slash of rain, the slice of December wind.

Etheldra stilled her hand above the cauldron as the three men burst into the cottage. Fat globs of mud fell from boots onto her clean floor, squared hats remaining atop three heads.

Rumors ran up and down the Cam faster than the punts that carried them. They had come.

"Where is she?"

Eltheldra reached up, gnarled fingers brushing against the dried rue and lavender, plucking a stick of rosemary with shaking hands. "I do not know," she said, picking off the leaves.

"The third girl since May Day," the oldest of the men said. He heaved in a breath, the buttons of his puritan's doublet stretching across the wide chest.

Etheldra worked at the mortar, the dried stalks of rosemary crushed beneath the pestle. The sharp scent rose through the cottage, masking the musk of sweat and horses. Rosemary for remembrance.

"And as I told you before, Master Hunter, I do not know what has become of them. I am a healer, as your wife well knew. I would never harm the girls of Cambridge." Girls like Jenni, for all the good her healing arts had proved.

Spittle ran down the stained jerkin of the other man, his beard wild. "Liar. Not seen at church these last ten years and more." A pause, dark and ominous as a gathering storm. "Witch."

Etheldra's face jerked up at the accusation. A dangerous word, after the tidings from Scotland last year. One she had waited months to hear.

"You took them," the man said. "You and your coven." Hate flashed in his eyes as he grinned. "I'll have you burned for what you've done to my Elizabeth."

The husband.

She should say nothing. This man expected his women to cower. But the Devil was in her, and the words slipped out. "What did you use this time, a knife?"

The man snarled, jumping like a maddened dog. Mad enough to slice his wife. What kind of a god put such men on his earth?

Master Hunter pulled at the man's jerkin, holding him back. "Master Thompson," he said to the third man, the one waiting just beneath the lintel. "Search this place."

The destruction was inevitable, she supposed. The chair and table overturned, herbs wrenched and scattered. The precious beeswax candles snapped in two, as if she might have a woman hidden inside.

The yard and the privy, the shed for the cow. As last time, they found no hint of the missing woman.

"She's already killed Elizabeth," the husband cried. "Witch. Murderer. Take her!"

But Hunter shook his head. "You must make your accusations to the magistrate, Goodman. We will come again, Goody Alter."

She understood.

Etheldra waited. Swept the floor with practiced hands as the hoofbeats departed, saving what she could. Surveyed the earthenware jars that lined her shelves, the work of a lifetime. Too many to bring, she thought, as the shadows of evening drew in on this longest night.

The settle, too, would have to stay. Etheldra ran her hand along the polished wood, traced the swirl of a carved arm. It had come from the monk's refectory, back in the days when England had such things. Did god live here then?

Now it was the bench where Jenni had taken her first little steps, where Matthew had sat after a long day in the fields. Where hundreds of women had crouched and told her of their troubles.

Who would tend Jenni's grave, once she had gone? Who would the women of Cambridge look to, for the wounds that wouldn't heal?

It was ever thus.

The drumming rain turned to a light mist, the night full dark when she finally ventured out. The dirt atop the cellar had turned to mud, and she struggled to lift the hatch.

"They have come and gone," Etheldra said. "It is safe enough."

But the girl could barely scramble up the few steps, her knees buckling as she crossed the yard.

Inside the packs were ready. Elizabeth sat at the table, picking at the heel of bread and cheese. Firelight danced off her flaxen hair, dully reflected in those glazed eyes.

Even as she unwrapped the bandage, Etheldra knew what she would find.

The girl had come too late. Scarlet skin puckered around the stitches in angry red welts, pink fingers trailing out from the wound despite the packed poultice. The poison spreading to her blood.

She was halfway to the next world already.

"Come and rest," Etheldra said, taking the sweat-soaked palm. "You have a long journey before you."

Outside the wind picked up, whistling through the chinks of the cottage as she finished her preparations. Shapes crept through the door, wraithlike. Cloaked in black. Encircling her.

When they were gathered, Etheldra removed her hood to reveal the greyed hair beneath. As grizzled as the once beautiful hands linked about her. She drank in the weathered faces, lined by years of grief and fear. She would miss them, when she was gone. These broken sisters.

The blade sliced cleanly through Elizabeth's flesh. A merciful end. A healing for the soul, if not the body.

Golden strands hissed as they met the fat of the cauldron, eyes sizzling like eggs frying in a pan.

"Tonight, will be the last," Etheldra said. "It has been my honor to worship with you."

Escape Plan - Amita Basu (she/her)

All morning I've waited for the sound, but when it comes, it startles me: wings fluttering below. Fifteen feet of masonry separate us but, with my face pressed to the bars, I can feel the warm down-scented breeze. I listen to the pair settling, picture their rose-pink feet dislodging dried pigeon shit. They begin cooing.

Coo, coo. Metronomic, tireless as the drip-drip of water on the scalp of that prisoner who was condemned to death from monotony. These birds could fly anywhere. They fly from the prison's west façade every morning to its east façade every afternoon.

I scratch another notch in my wall calendar.

I count the rice grains I saved from dinner and dried in this morning's patch of sunshine as it crawled across my floor. Twenty-three. I add them to the dried rice I've hidden in the hollowed leg of my bed—not that anyone ever comes in here to clean. I've got 3,547 grains of rice. I need more. I'll only get one chance.

Coo, coo. I always hated pigeons. Only after coming here did I understand why.

I remember pigeons flocking to the birdseed that wiry old jogger in Company Garden used to scatter. In the sun, their throats iridescing blue-violet, they're almost beautiful.

Sometimes a white pigeon wanders into the dull-gray flock. Do pigeons recognise a belle, and woo her, as the tour guides on Benaras banks woo a white girl with unbound hair and meat-fed shoulder muscles?

Here, on the top floor, the heat is stupefying. My windowsill is narrow, offering the delicate pigeons no shade. The windows on the lower storeys must be shaded. I wasn't paying attention when they brought me here—I felt sure I'd be out soon. I remember glimpsing, that smoggy February, a straggling hodgepodge building, half stone, half brick, the odd pale face peering between the bars.

Coo, coo. Why don't they get bored? Even mediocre flyers could soar across India, stage by stage. Messenger birds were pigeons. Why don't these birds fly away?

The bell rings. Footsteps shuffle out to the yard for exercise hour. I used to envy the downstairs prisoners. But can you imagine glimpsing the outside world, then being marched back into darkness? I'm better off here, staring at my square of sky that goes from dark-gray to light-gray, light-gray to dark-gray.

I recount my notches. 109 days left till my tenth anniversary here. I'm planning a little treat.

Ten days beforehand, I'll start paving my windowsill with rice grains. Let the pigeons get comfortable, peck-peck, draw them a little closer each day. How tender they smell under their wings, like a puppy—slightly moist, like an infant—just weaned. On my anniversary I'll wait till a pigeon swollen with rice turns its back to me to doze. Flashing out between the bars my hand to wring the beastie's neck. It will peck me, and draw blood, and leave scars.

That's how I'll know it really happened, that something's happened at last, that I'm not trapped in limbo, hallucinating one endless day.

Goody Wright of Stradbroke - Emma Wells (she/her)

They've started to bring their dead to me—to my herb-rich grassland. A pile of quicklime-licked corpses wink at me from the kitchen window, overt as unsheathed blades, stacked in a macabre pile next to the village dung heap. A dung heap that steams with the stench of disregard. I cast away, frown, allowing sadness to soak into places where hollows echo. Holes of me that resist companionship, loyalty from the living or due deference for my skilled trade. All are absent—barred for the likes of me. A village witch. An oddity.

I have lived on the periphery of Stradbroke in Suffolk since my birth—born in the very countryside hovel that I still abide within. Moving is tricky, dangerous. There are always others tracking my path, listening for dark whisperings in the night, hoping to know of any planned stirrings from my unofficial post. I'm both wanted and repelled as a cunning woman: called for in times of life and death but ostracised at all others.

When villagers bumble along contentedly, which is the most part of life, not requiring a healing poultice nor herbal tincture to ease their suffering and woes, I am unseen, a mute. I live both inside and outside of this life, yet they would hate my leaving of them for another county. For, I am shunned, worthless in the judgement of the majority of villagers, until utter need alerts them, urging them to my door.

Need comes pressingly when it calls, exactingly, especially for the birthing of awkward babes. Breech—the position all mothers fear as an inverted Christian cross hung upon a door, advertising the practice of devilment within a building's unholy walls.

Lamentably, I have lost count of the eggshell blue faces of babes that I have cut loose from dying women, hanging on peripheries of life; purplish bruised cords hoping to strangle free breath from fragile, tiny and brittle throats as quivering fledglings. Breech births are an enemy to my practice. Too many eye me with disdain, questioning if I have brought doom to village doors with my misunderstood methods and perceived webs of darkling art—this is always the case if mother and babe cannot be saved. Both lives are crushed quaking grass or purplish flowers, papery, trembling upon slender, hair-like stalks.

Fathers are useless, viewing birth as "women's work", absenting themselves from homes to local inns until the wailing stops—sometimes sounds stop perpetually on their eventual return, when I cannot turn misplaced, adamant feet of babes in time or if the mother has already bled out, dying crimson what were once bleached white sheets, kneaded by dutiful wives or maidservants, purging linens of sinful human smears.

I know that these blood-drained women will beckon soundlessly at my cottage door when they have been brought here as deadened sacks on a cart, for they are building a cemetery out of my herb garden. Once, only wheat fields punctuated with wildflowers, was my horizontal view: ox-eye daisies, yellow rattle, fairy flax and birds-foot trefoil. A place of nature. Peace.

Village dwellers being too far off, pleasingly so, care not at all for my peripheral placement on the edge of other's livelihoods. They think I'm stupid and have yet to quicken with the thought that the church graveyard in the village overspills, and that they seek wider, unclaimed land to bury their dead, twining with the soil as ivy. Nobody has asked for my permission. Nobody cares to do so. My voice, even if uttered, will be soundless, mirroring the chill that tightens around decaying corpses as a wispy shroud whilst winter months trudge onwards, completing a seasonal journey.

Comparable to harvest, as the farmer ploughs the fields of wheat, separating wheat from sheaf, my head too wobbles on a precarious stalk. I feel a steely scythe whisper to my flesh, ready to behead, cutting my remedial knowledge clean from this world, in one fell swoop of a sharpened blade.

The latest scandal is that I am trading the Devil's imps for payment. Village talk is that I will hang and then burn in Bury St Edmunds for my crimes—there shall be no fire escape or exit from pain. It is said that I keep toads as familiars, the Devil's spirit animals, in clay pots which I release in the abyss of night to curse my enemies within the village: maiming skin with wasting diseases; blighting cattle; and cursing newborns with disfigurement. They envision me foraging along ditches for henbane and poison ivy, carrying portable death back in jars, quick to stopper breath of enemy villagers.

Elizabeth Greene is my current accuser. Mere tittle-tattle aggrandises itself until the likes of Mathew Hopkins rotates my name in his unhallowed mouth as an unspent sovereign. It is utter lunacy—nothing more, but regardless, a fever sweeps East Anglia with Hopkins at the helm of the crusade against so-called witches. A hologram of misjudged malevolence stalks his each, and every, footfall.

Elizabeth's real issue is that the sale of her husband's charms to protect against witches make a sharp decline when I manage to cure an ailment; turn a stubborn breech babe, save its mother or heal afflicted skin. For those that meet me, call for my aid, invite me into homes, discern for themselves, that in truth, I am no witch.

Her husband sells Bellarmine bottles to guard off "the Devil's whores", filled with human hair, iron nails, urine, pointed sticks and nail clippings. My healing, when I am not accused of witchcraft, has caused their power to deplete, and so they, both husband and wife, want me killed so their heathen charms can be sold more lucratively. They are willing to trade my life, the life of a wise healer, for a screwy bottle of piss that will do nothing to keep the likes of the Devil at bay.

True evil, the truest form, lies in the eyes of Matthew Hopkins who rounds elderly women as withered sheep deemed fit for slaughter. Evil lies in the mind of the Greenes, my false accusers, and in the gaze of a man's eyes who thinks it is right to force himself upon the flesh of a woman. Evil resides within twists of the knotted noose that shall silhouette my head—that is evil, all are so, but not I. Never I.

Stradbroke gossip chitter-chatters of my impending doom. A noose is strung and ready to be tied in Bury St Edmunds which is where I shall meet my final breath. A ticking clock is a siren call to my demise, mirroring the drooping, fallen heads of ox-eye daisies, once large ochre discs turned to dying suns.

As drab curtains close upon my final days and nights alive, a new malevolence creeps its vines within the makeshift cemetery that grows around my cottage. Grave robbers. Keen-sensed they have snuffled out a new charnel house for the local dead and come here in steely night to thieve corpses for high doctor's fees. No Bellarmine jars of protection or buried dead cats or witches' circles shall protect the dead from their hungry, money-grabbing fingers. This is evil. Not my cures. My midwifery. My tinctures, creams and salves. None kill.

That is not, nor was ever, my purpose.

Pallid, rotting corpses continue to be tossed in a heap above my herbal garden, crushing cures, pressing petals to useless pulp underneath the heavy weight of decay and curdling rot.

***

Wintery morning arrives of my trial and foretold hanging, and I bid farewell to my herbal kitchen, brim-full with tonics for the sick. Each healing jar blinks away a sharpened tear, hot, metallic, like the slash of an executioner's axe. As my lame, weathered feet shuffle to the door, I eye two familiar but deadened faces from the heap of the newly arrived dead. Molly, and her stillborn babe, breech, cursed in the womb by an unseeing God. I could not turn her baby boy in time nor stopper the determined river of scarlet from between Molly's quivering legs.

Both were lost to God only a few days ago in the village. Their shuttered eyes bid me on to meet them—on the other side of this unfair, cruel and blinding life that dims for me by the minute. I nod silently, agreeing to their silent call, in an unknown place, where perhaps our souls can be saved and our hope redeemed. As I cross their path, I pick a clutch of forget-me-nots, placing the small floral heads on the mother's chest—the darkling blue matches her breathless skin. Shuttering away emotion, I traipse on, to face my accusers.

One waits for me on the high road.

Hopkins.

As he scans me coldly, Hopkins jumps from a horse-drawn coach, eager to lock me within his ghastly hunt of wrongful condemnation. A brew that is red-hot, burning to the touch, scalding innocent skin laid bare. His long cloak swishes in the November breeze, and as it does so, I see the devil-thronged tail of his sins, licking like a devilish tongue, poking freely from the cloaked folds of sable sheep's wool, too eager to savour the taste of my death. A devilish smirk wrinkles upon his face, as his pendulum forked tongue, swings back and forth, counting out my remaining days and hours alive.

The coach speeds onwards, enclosing me in its shrinking walls, as I hear church bells toll below a skyline of stormy slate. The bell is a summons to greet death, face-to-face, as I finger a plaited weave of cowslip in my quaking fingers, praying it is my key to heaven, and St Peter will welcome me into his spectral flock. I shuffle awkwardly in my seat, knowing that this is only the start of my torment.

Stealthily, the coach ploughs on, effacing my existence with each turn of its clanking wheels. I glance down, accepting my fate: the blighted fate of an accused "cunning woman".

Mary of the Chance Encounters - Margaret Elysia Garcia (she/her)

On Saturdays, Anthony goes to the drive-in and breathes in the ghosts of a time he's never been a part of. His favorite drive-in is empty six days out of the week and no longer home to movies on Friday nights. These days, it is just a vacant lot with rusted poles and white-chipped boxes with metal hooks that once held speakers and now hold nothing at all. Archeological markers where the cars and teens once parked.

One Saturday a month was the antique swap meet on one side of the lot. The rest of the Saturdays it was vendors from all over bringing in the most horrendous knock-offs from Mexico and China to sell on top of folding tables and blue tarps. Action figures whose face paints were slightly off—enough to imprint eyes where the eyebrows should be and asymmetrical noses. The toys, in particular, looked frightening.

But on the other side of the swap meet they sold antiques and camera equipment. Not just any camera equipment, but Polaroids of all eras. Sometimes a stout Russian woman from Odessa would sell unopened boxes of Polaroid film out of a Coleman cooler. She always looked at Anthony suspiciously and he couldn't tell whether she suspected him of something or if that was just her nature. He often asked her where she got her merchandise and she just smiled exposing a couple missing teeth.

Anthony parked on a side street nearby and limbo-rocked himself under the metal chain and made his way to the antique stalls, the saint candle vendor, and the cameras.

Anthony made a point of touching the speaker boxes as he passed as if they were holy water basins. He sometimes made the sign of the cross. They were prayers to the past—perhaps, the essence of film itself trapped inside.

His life felt like a series of things that once were and were no more. He screened his first movies at the La Mirada Mall, which closed down when he was still in high school. He used to do the martial arts double features at the Hadley, but then it closed for remodeling and reopened as a pharmacy. There was the dollar movie theater by the old Alpha Beta but that turned into a Planet Fitness gym. The Alpha Beta became a Gigante! His aunts were happy to see a mercado they were familiar with in the neighborhood, but Anthony stuck to Trader Joe's. It had been there thirty years and didn't look like anything would change.

His father used to stop at that Alpha Beta on the way to the cemetery. He'd stop and buy pink carnations to bring to the grave of Anthony's mother at Calvary Cemetery in East LA. His mother was buried in the same area of the cemetery as film stars. She rested not too far from the Barrymores, Pola Negri, and his favorite, Ramon Navarro. Navarro he thought was a lot like him. Or he was a lot like Navarro, his skin, his accent making it nearly impossible for him to be considered completely one thing or the other. He appreciated Navarro's mannerisms. His reserve. His quiet. His almost passing.

He loved sitting next to poor Kathryn Adams in Calvary. He sometimes brought her flowers too. She wasn't too far from his mother who had always enjoyed her silent films. Kathryn, she thought, should have had a longer career. By 1925, she was already done. His mother had wanted to be a movie star and she had been cast as a maid several times. A love interest once. A prostitute. She wanted a vamp part along the lines of Theda Bara, but never got one. She looked too matronly, too supporting actress, too stocky to be a vamp.

But Anthony's mother had been beautiful; she belonged with the silent film stars. If she'd been with them she'd have one of those giant concrete statues of an angel or Jesus residing over her in Calvary. The kind of statues where Mexi-Goth kids come and paint the stone fingernails black. Expansive wings could have taken her in and protected her in a way she could not be protected on Earth. They could have provided her safe passage to the world beyond. Beyond the world of talkies and cancer.

His mother had died too young, her late 30s. She left him boxes of movie trinkets and posters she'd collected. Her scrapbooks weren't photos of people he knew in the family, but of the one's she felt the closest affinity for—movie stars of a forgotten era. He was glad that they buried her at Calvary among the dead sirens of the screen.

Anthony thought of her as he thumbed through film memorabilia at one of the stalls. He loved the story of how he was born. Though they lived in Montebello, they went back to visit family in Mexico while his mother was pregnant with him. His mother was feeling woozy that day and went to the movies to settle herself; it had been a western. They joked he must have come three months early because he wanted to watch the show. They were American citizens by then, but they had to sneak Anthony across. They had to be back at work; there was no time for proper papers. Anthony spoke no Spanish but was undocumented for the first sixteen years of his life. Anthony remembered going back and forth. He was always too shy to speak.

Anthony smiled at the man in the record bin booth who was trying to convince him to start collecting 78s. He looked through them politely but inquired about nothing.

"There's nothing quite like a 78! You need to get a player. I could get one for you, eh?" said the man in the gold-rimmed glasses and bad toupee. He put on Bing Crosby for him. "I have jazz too if you like that sort of thing," he said. Anthony noticed a woman in the booth next to the 78s man. She and her wares looked better suited for a steampunk convention. Every inch of the booth was covered in rusty contraptions and all textiles had lace or buttons, corsets. It was like he was looking into an entirely other world.

The woman caught his eye; she sat in the middle of the booth on a chaise lounge rather than a folding chair. She looked ready for a vintage sepia photo shoot, as if she were a silent film star come to life. Her dress was a billowy mass of beaded and sequined silk. She had leather granny boots that laced up to her knee. Her lips were deep red and her eye makeup was smoky and dark.

"Do you ever feel you were born in the wrong era? Or that you are walking around in the wrong decade?" she asked, extending her hand. At first Anthony did not touch it but she kept it extended and he remembered his manners and kissed the top of her hand. She smiled and withdrew it after.

"All the time," said Anthony.

"And who is this that has come to court me?" She winked her left eye at him. She looked a little like Kathryn Adams with just a dash of Dolores del Rio. He was enchanted.

"My name is Anthony," he said, "Anthony Calera."

"Ah! Yes. Calera."

"You know me? Us?"

"Who in East LA does not know the story of your grandfather? It is a great legend."

"What story?" Anthony was beginning to get a bit freaked out.

"Why the goat story. Of course." Anthony stood there amazed. He didn't say a word.

"You don't know the story of your own grandfather? Well such is the case of so many children today. Happy to know the stories of Hollywood, when the best action and suspense is right in their very backyards. Here. I'll tell you," she said. Anthony sat down on the side of her chaise lounge and looked intently at her. There were always cousins and tías in southern California he didn't know. It was quite plausible she was one of them. Didn't they have some family in San Pedro? More in Pomona? It made him sad to think at times that the family who'd come over from Mexico together dispersed upon arrival in California and along with the language, had become so alien to each other.

"The story went like this," she said. He listened. He knew only the vague outline of what she was about to tell him and if she did know his grandfather's story, she could fill in where generations had placed silence.

"The story goes something like this. Your grandmother was bored of the grandfather—and they were still young—she in her twenties and he in his thirties. She'd given birth to your father six months before and her body had not gotten back to itself. Your grandfather took to going into town after sundown to the cantina to cry in his beer. His young bride was already not what he wanted. Too old before her time.

Now your grandmother spent her day gardening and sewing and cooking for your grandfather, but when he went down for naps in the afternoon, she began sleeping with the two men your grandfather had hired to work his land while he went to town. They say it had been going on many months and that she was probably pregnant with another baby when your grandfather caught her naked in bed with both men at once in the middle of some sinful act—in the loudness of it where one can hear no cries of babies, no anguish of husbands.

Your grandfather went to his study and took out his gun. He kicked open the door and shot all three of them dead in his own bed. You could still do that in Mexico then. It was a crime of passion. It was how lesser men revenged a broken heart. They were always acquitted. Infidelity. Ecstasy. Gunpowder. Your father was only six months old and not quite weaned. Your grandfather sent for a nanny and a goat and made arrangements for them to move to Los Angeles.

Your grandmother had been born in the United States; he brought her back and interred her at Calvary. Your grandfather never returned to Mexico again, not even to visit his own family. He bought a ranch out in Pomona. He bought dairy goats and employed a nanny full-time and eventually married her. Your father's primos made fun of him and called him chivas—the kid of the goat. Your grandfather moved to East Los Angeles when he was too old to ranch with his son and his second wife, your Mama. On Fridays he took your Mama to the movies. They moved to Whittier when they got a little money. That's where you live, little Anthony, correct? That's the story.

"The plot in Calvary Cemetery where they buried your grandmother—your real grandmother—was cheap and near the curb. The curb where they bury homeboys with black and white recent photos of them in hairnets and gold crosses and inscriptions on headstones that read May Our Lady Watch Over Our Beloved. They are always beloved of their mothers. Those mothers lose them to cholas, cheap beer, and drugs. But the children lose their mothers too, don't they?"

The lady patted Anthony's knee. He must have looked rather startled. He'd only heard there had been a shooting. That his grandmother had died on the ranch. Probably killed by revolutionaries stealing through the fields. He'd never heard this version before. He did know there was a goat though, it just never made sense before. I mean, not that it made a good deal of sense now.

"My name is Mary, my dear Anthony," said the woman.

"How do you know all this? Are you a tía? Do you always come to the swap meet to sell steampunk gadgets and tell people horrific tales of their families? What happened to the two men?" Anthony searched her face for familiar features. He wouldn't know his grandmother's people much, but if she was from his grandfather's side he'd certainly see it in her cheekbones or her eyes. "I'd like to take a photograph of you. Do you mind?"

"Oh that would be lovely," Mary said, "but I'm afraid I brought no mirror with me. Let me run to the ladies' room a moment and fix myself properly for such a thing. And who knows about the two men? Make up a story. It will do."

"Just as you are is fine," said Anthony. He wondered if the descendants of the two men also had strange women in swap meets telling them tales. Mary got up from the chaise and shook her head, determined to look the way she wanted to look for the photograph. She straightened the imbroglio she wore around her neck. Anthony searched his bag for his Polaroid. He wished he'd brought a more old fashioned camera to photograph her. But he hadn't. Then he remembered in his trunk was an older camera from the forties that developed on five by seven film. He'd put it in the car for a photo shoot last weekend that never materialized.

"Mary, you go freshen up. I'm going to get my other camera," Anthony told her as she was rushing off. Mary turned and took his hand.

"It's so lovely to finally meet you," she said.

"Finally?" She smiled at him and walked towards the restrooms. Anthony dashed away to his car and carried the equipment as quickly back to the booth as he could. When he returned he stood there confused. The 78s seller to the left was still there and on the right of him where Mary's booth had been was a stall of mid-century modern furniture. The silent movie memorabilia was gone. Mary was gone. Only the chaise lounge remained unadorned, without its lace, and looking oddly conspicuous among the 1950s Danish pieces.

"Did you see what happened to the booth here? To the lady I was speaking with? In the steampunk costume?" he asked of the 78s seller. The man looked at him rather peculiar.

"Son, nothing has been in the booth all day. The seller hasn't even shown back up since we opened. Three people asked about that chaise lounge too. It's a shame." Anthony looked all around the stall at all the furniture: sleek wood tables, buffets, chairs, the chaise. In the corner was a vase of peacock feathers in a green vase on top of an art nouveau secretary's desk with ornate legs. He found a bible, a pair of white feathers like writing quills, and Thomas Brother's Guide of Los Angeles from 1945. He found a locket next to it with the same imbroglio Mary had straightened as she headed to the restroom. He opened it. Inside was a photo of Mary.

He placed twenty dollars on the secretary's desk, shoved her in his front pocket and walked quickly away from the stall.

NON FICTION

spirit of the woods 45th annual – andrea lianne grabowski
(she/her)

> *"community care is only real if we both offer to create it and to accept it" —raechel anne jolie*

six months & eight days since we last saw one another, & the festival grounds drape small & cozy over the dry grass. my mind stumbles, coalesces the atoms & angles of your face into the full picture, & my chest shoots up in the dust.

i turn.

focus on the zip ties in my aunt's hands. the signs we're hanging. anything but you hauling speakers & hooking wires. duct tape is bitter & my teeth can't tear it. i would hang this welcoming rainbow sign with scientific precision. i would leave it sloppy & find the gate in four seconds.

how could i not have guessed you might be here? almost as if i've forgotten who you are. if i ever knew. you're in skinny jeans; i've rested my hand on that worn pleated blue, know the kind of softness it holds. i'm in the same high-waisted light denim i wore that december night in the co-op, when our tears fell on gluten-free lemon shortbread & you said it was real, us being everything, until you realized that kind of thing was bad for you.

my family & i have other places to be but we are coming back—i have never been to this festival before & i want this, i want this. you & i used to diminish folk music, & will i ever get to tell you how much i listen to it now? my uncle & aunt drive us past sagging farmhouses with deliciously flaking paint & i drop pins on google maps. i don't want to go back to them alone. would i want to with you? like we did so often?

the heavy rain in my muscles is answer enough.

*

i don't see you in the crowds & i wonder if it's wrong of me to wish i did. like chasing the panic, like the spike of adrenaline when we were caught in february night traffic on grandview parkway. your old truck i never drove, & my car you sat behind the wheel of countless times. but instead, yarn is snarled out in front of me & i'm teaching a child whose name is a season how to weave scarlet wool across a warp of blue. he chooses gold, more blue. we untangle strands, & then, you're standing at the edge of the activity gazebo,

& i still think you are beautiful, & these feelings are still like spilled tar on my neurotransmitters,

& the season-child is twisting the yarn backwards. i kneel on the concrete to let his mother block me from your sight, to hide in the tie-dye sparkle of his smile, to guide his hands forward with the tapestry needle. but i still hope you saw me.

*

i sit cross-legged on my aunt's blanket. you're in the sound tent some meters away. my heart isn't shooting up anymore. there's a seven-year-old in my lap & her face is painted with a sunflower. her mother & my aunts are cheering for the two musicians on the stage: hearth & hymn gifting us with folk ballads & a water protectors' anthem.

the next song begins as an apology. i allow myself

a glance at you, & you heft the black backpack i know just as well as my own. the exterior, not the contents. i'd let you rifle around in mine any day. sometimes you pulled your sketchbook from yours & slipped me a gift, showed me nearly every new page.

forgive me.[1] the bittersweet tune slides through the crowd. *for all the times i never had the guts to.*

your backpack is stitched in patches i gave you when we traded tentative secrets & held each other in the depths of michigan winter. *for all the ways i could've held your hand but i didn't.* the one with the lit match, some words about creation, not destruction. & the one with the purple flowers: i'll save myself embroidered in gothic lettering.

the song weaves something like atonement, for abandoned listening & nights like the ones i texted you & trembled at my empty screen. *what are the ways that we know how to love?*

i could ask that kind of question all day:
bloodlines.   neighbors.   friendship.queerness.undefined.

how we always stop ourselves. you don't like music this soft. the sun-girl's little brother is screeching. i hope he gets your attention, i hope you glance over & see me here like this. i hope you see me flanked by a moment of protection, or abundance, or something not like scarcity.

the song weaves apology for futile intimacy. my chin rests lightly on the sun-girl's snarled cornsilk curls. *everything you wanted felt like not me.* if i cannot hear you actualize the kind of eloquence you used to laud me for, then let me hear what i needed to hear from

you through the tender words of another, while you are as close to me as perhaps you ever want to be again.

you can make a habit out of anything. i have the purple flowers patch too, tried to save myself over & over again. was that because you believed salvation occurred in isolation? i don't know. it's like the song is saying—everything we ever tried to do with our love was messy. until, for you, i don't think it was even love at all. over the tear-stained shortbread, you said, "there is nothing wrong with you." did those words come too late?

i tried to save myself over & over & over again, & maybe i finally
have.

or maybe this song has.
& the trees,   & stinging nettles,   & the lake wind,
& no cell service,   & yarn,   & the trees.

your hair's grown long again. it looks good. mine has too. i like it this
way. you're still in dark hues, like we both used to restrict ourselves
to. a lullaby drifts from the stage. the sun-girl is almost asleep, head
curled into the parchment knit-mesh of my sleeve. my earrings are
the color of her face paint. her mother's dress is like coral & she
guides new life into the world. my aunt's shirt is like spruce needles
at the height of summer. could i go a week without wearing black?
the emcee makes us cheer for the sound team,

& so, i do. after all, this is what you are best at: wires, switches,
everyone else's noise, your silence. & this is what i do best: the story
of what is inside me.

the motions of your hands are no stranger as you adjust the
beekeeper's mic for the next act. i have known the beekeeper since
before i was born: my father mended his trucks, my mother walked
past with a tray of candles & a gleam in her eyes. do you remember
that story, remember how my family is woven into this place?

maybe you'll listen to newhaven or hollywood undead on the way
home. i'll pick lullaby bangers, then a bit of ethel cain; i'll pick every
soft girl you might never care for, like me, like me.

---

[1]*all italicized lyrics from "Habits" by Elisabeth Pixley-Fink. permission for use
granted by the artist.*

Am I really bi-sexual or have I just been possessed by a demon? – Bleah Patterson (she/her)

When we get on the dating site, change the settings from "woman interested in men; age 25-42" to "woman interested in women; age 18-30," we know we're already off to a bad start. Why is it creepy for us to date a man who's frontal lobe isn't fully developed but not a woman? Why are we not attracted to women who might have the beginnings of laugh lines, or are more likely to have a kid now? Is this some sort of internalized misogyny? We tell ourselves that no one needs to know the settings we place on Hinge or Bumble or OkCupid—does anyone even still use OkCupid anymore, or is it just for sex trafficking and selling feet pics?—But then we tell ourselves that if we ever become a senator, or a top executive, or even more elusive: get a book deal, we could definitely get canceled for this—but then again we'd probably get canceled for the homophobic blog posts at twelve, comparing being gay to being a murderer, before anyone figured out how to hack our Bumble account.

We have a note saved on our phones to copy and paste into any conversations that start to feel promising. We try not to make it obvious that it's scripted and pepper the note with emojis that are awkward, humble, and optimistic for a spur-of-the-moment sort of authenticity. We think that we definitely must actually be bisexual because don't women always move fast with other women? And forty-five minutes into messaging we pull out the pre-approved dialogue:

Hey so I'm really enjoying talking to you [insert heart eyes emoji here]! But I wanted to get something out of the way before we get too far [that grin and bear it sort of smiling emoji here, for self-awareness]. The thing is, I've never been with a girl before—

We erase the word girl, replace it with woman. Good catch. We prefer to be called a girl, it seems more authentic and genuine to where we are in our lives—not at all put together and hopefully not in any sort of final iteration—and we've also got all of those lingering daddy issues. But we've noticed that other ~~girls~~—women— don't like being called girls at all.

—I've never been with a woman before and I'm kind of just now exploring that side of my sexuality. I won't bore you with the details, lol [insert nervous smiling emoji with the sweat drop above its head here] but TL;DR: religious trauma, compulsive heterosexuality, and self-loathing [tongue out laughing emoji]. Anyway! I just like to put that out there right away so you can, you know, make the decision if it's worth your time. Totally understand if not, no worries! [insert pink heart emoji here]

The message sprawls the length of the phone screen and then some, we make a mental note to see if we can tighten it later so it doesn't look like a page from a novel. And then comes the waiting, there's always a period of waiting. But that's preferred because we've learned that if they respond too quickly, it means they just want to get laid but we're not there yet. It took us seven years after we lost our virginity to be okay with just getting laid with a guy and we've still never done anything but makeout with a (straight, drunk) girl. So we unmatch with them and try again. Like those word generators that help us out of writer's block, you just roll again and hope for the best.

Her: Don't take this personally

Her: I just gotta make sure you don't have like

Her: a boyfriend and y'all are trying to spice things up

Her: save your relationship or whatever

We respond that we're definitely not taking it personally at all and that's totally fair [lol, smiley face], but that no we're totally single and haven't been in a relationship (it was a guy, just so we're clear) for two years. And this is mostly true, we haven't been Facebook official or living with our ex, or telling our close friends or parents that we're dating in two years. He picks us up to go on a date—where we pay, or we go dutch—every couple weeks, he spends the night, and then we usually cry and say we just want things to go back to normal and he leaves abruptly and it's a month or two of radio silence until he's horny again and ready to forget the whole thing. We're on one of those lulls right now and our coworker, Laura, says that we really need to put ourselves out there and that if we find someone else we won't feel like we need to keep taking what little he has to offer anymore. We think that's pretty good if not kind of depressing advice. "You should finally try girls," she said as if they're guacamole or salmon and we're only mildly offended and keenly aware that it's because the internet told us to be, "You're always talking about how cute and nice they are. You deserve nice, you deserve to know if you really like them too." Laura's the straight girl we made out with while she was drunk at a party and it's our little secret now that she's married and we're the only friend her husband doesn't hate.

Her: Okay :) Well that doesn't bother me at all!

Her: I've been dating women for a long time now.

Her: I haven't dated a guy since highschool.

Her: Why do you think you've waited so long to explore? <3

Me: Honestly? I always make the joke that I'm terrified and disgusted by my own body, lol. So why would I want to interact with someone who had a body as scary and gross as mine?

She doesn't respond for a long time, we get an eerily familiar feeling that she might never respond or at least, whatever she'll eventually say might as well be a non-response.

When we were four years old our grandma told us that if we wore our pants below our belly buttons they would fall off and we'd die. Told us never to spend too long washing "down there." Caught us— after we'd gotten our first padded bra earlier than all of our friends, at eleven—pulling our pajama shirt taut in the bathroom mirror to see our own shape, told us to stop acting like a whore. We were determined though, to learn about our body and the bodies of our Barbies and Polly Pockets and even our friend's bodies, obsessed with the idea that a woman was like a Pandora's box and if you opened her up you might never get to put back the horrors that escaped.

That is, until we were twelve at sleepover and our best friend asked us if we knew what a period was and we said something like, "You mean the thing at the end of a sentence? Come on Brooke, I'm homeschooled, not stupid." She smirked, meanly in a way we'd only ever seen her smirk at the other girls who weren't our friends. "No, like, the thing that makes you a woman. So you can have babies." Babies. We'd always wondered about babies.

When we'd asked our grandma where babies come from she said True Love's Kiss. When we asked how your body knows the difference between a regular kiss and True Love's Kiss she reminded us about Sleeping Beauty and Snow White and Ariel and said it was the same and we believed her but were still curious of the mechanics of it all. Kissing truly, lovingly.

Brooke told us that when you get your period you bleed and it hurts, that you have to wear a pad or it'll stain your clothes and never come out and everyone will laugh at you and also you'll spread disease. We were enraptured, we'd never been allowed to say the word 'fart' or 'pee' or 'butt' and television and movies for kids that relished in jokes about bodily functions were strictly forbidden. The idea that these things would happen to our body, and that Brooke knew all about them fascinated us. She took out paper and colored pencils and drew a naked man—not boy, he had hair all over—and a woman, who surprisingly had no hair at all. We made a mental note that men had hair and women did not, how interesting. One thing led into another and we sat criss-cross-applesauce on her bed, us at the foot and her at the head, with our own papers and pencils filling out questionnaires we'd created about our wedding night like those MASH games we played when we were supposed to be listening to the sermon at church.

WHO: Jesse McCartney

WEDDING SONG: I Want Candy, (obviously)

WHERE:

We asked Brooke, "Like 'where' in a bed or like 'where' in Bermuda?" She responded, "Up to you, don't overthink it."

WHERE: In a big fluffy bed in Paris overlooking the Eiffel Tower

WHAT WILL YOU WEAR (DRAW!):

We felt nervous, we don't know where we'd seen lingerie before—maybe in one of our grandmother's daytime soaps—or what our idea of it was—if a skirt above the knees, a shoulder, some cleavage could cause a man to stumble, what different sensation does a thin, lace, nightgown provide?—but we drew a woman in a lacy bra attached and matching lacy panties that looked kind of like a diaper, and beneath those we attached garters and we felt a shiver run up and down our body. Brooke switched papers with us, and together we giggled at our answers. And then we were tired, crashing after too many Capri Suns, and we put the papers under the bed and fell asleep tangled under her Hannah Montana or High

School Musical comforter. We didn't think about kissing Brooke, for the record.

The next morning her mom woke us up and promptly said it was time to go home, our grandma was on the way. We were confused but also still uncomfortable with sleepovers, so we packed our things and waited on the living room sofa. When our grandma arrived she was red in the face with wet puddles on her squishy, high cheeks. "Do you want to tell me, or are you going to lie about it like a little bitch?" Our stomach sank. We thought about every bad thing we had ever done: taken communion without asking Jesus to forgive our sins, playing MASH instead of taking sermon notes, looking at the answer-key for our math homework, stealing the tag off of a Webkinz at Hallmark so that we could play the computer game, saying "stupid" under our breath just to try it out. "I don't know what you're talking about, what happened?" She made a laughing noise mixed with a screaming noise. "Brooke's mom told me what you did." We realized that we'd forgotten all about the night before, sleepy and drunk on sugar. "We were just playing, like, pretend. We weren't doing anything bad." Our grandma wasn't having it, "She showed me what you drew. Garters? Really? Talking about S-E-X? What is wrong with you, why would you want to talk about something so disgusting?"

We ended up in the Pastor's office, Brooke pinned the whole thing on me and her mom said we were possessed by a demon of lust and perversion. "I can't stay in this church knowing this kind of influence is going to be around my family," she sobbed. The Pastor looked tired, he sighed. "What do you want done?" he asked. "I want them thrown out." My grandma was crying, she ran the ladies brunches and the food pantry and taught a Sunday school class on etiquette, organized the Fall Festivals and the Backpack Giveaways and had single handedly painted all of the stage props and made all of the costumes for last year's Christmas play. "That's a little too far," the Pastor said. We looked at Brooke with daggers and she looked back at us smugly. "What about a therapist?" the Pastor asked, "Can she go see a therapist and try to make sure there's nothing going on she needs to talk about?" Brooke's mom huffed loudly, "She doesn't need therapy, she needs this demon cast out of her body!" The Pastor seemed to roll his eyes, he walked over to his desk and took out a small bottle of holy oil and turned it upside down dabbing both of his thumbs. He sat on the edge of his desk in front of us and put oil on both of our temples and asked us to close our eyes. He began to pray in tongues and we began to cry, feeling overwhelmed and tired and nervous. "How do you feel?" he asked us as we sobbed, "Better?" We nodded. He looked up to Brooke's mom and then at my grandma, "I'm going to recommend therapy, until then I don't think she should be back in church." And then he looked back to Brooke's mom, "Fair?" She nodded reluctantly. "Sure, and she's never allowed to speak to my Brooke or my family ever again." "Fine," we said, glaring at Brooke. And our grandma dragged us out by our ear.

We swiped left and right, though mostly right—we found women so much more beautiful than we'd ever found men, men only become beautiful once you've seen them smile or laugh or cry or speak passionately about something or fall in love with you— until we reached our limit, we refused to pay for unlimited swipes because that was something desperate people did and we were not desperate, just curious. We went to sleep. In the morning we woke up to matches, not as many as if they had been men, but a couple and we decided that we would message them first.

Me: First, can I just say you're beautiful.

We copy and pasted this to all of them and it was still not untrue.

Me: Secondly, I want to apologize in advance. I'm a little exhausted by this online dating thing, or rather... the preliminary part, since I haven't met anyone who actually wants to date me yet.

I'll just come out and say it: I've never been with a woman, but I've loved a couple and I've always wanted to. I was just scared. I'm done being scared. I'm a good partner and a good girlfriend, you don't have to be a guy for me to love you or care about you. But I'm afraid of the sex part, because it's new and because I was just raised with so much shame... anyway... I'm sorry for the rambling. I won't be mad if this isn't worth exploring for you, I just didn't want to get my hopes up and disappoint us both later.

We were trying to accept that this is who we were: a woman who loved men but had been hurt by so many. And someone who'd loved women more than we'd ever loved men... or... differently than we'd ever loved men, and wanted to see if we could be a better partner to them and find a better partner with them, in that world of loving a woman. We still didn't know which part of us is the demon. We'd assumed for so long it was the part that wanted to kiss a girl but we weren't sure now and we weren't sure anymore that it mattered.

[a letter] [to remain unsent] – andrea lianne grabowski (she/her)

i went with silvia into the tunnels that catch & filter the desert rains tonight. armed with head lamps, fueled with ▮▮▮▮▮▮ batteries & cans of spray paint stowed in her backpack & a water bottle, we slip below a hole in a fence marked ▮▮▮▮▮▮▮▮. part of me wishes you were here. the other part of me tells silvia, *what i miss the most is* ▮▮▮▮ *was the only person up north who i could explore with.*

there is no fear in my movements. silvia jumps from concrete into scrubby, littered land something like five feet below & flips up a shitty old fridge. i sit at the edge of the concrete & slip onto the fridge she's holding steady, since i am too short to jump, & well, okay, a little scared. how much harder would it have been for you to jump, how much easier to keep it together & look cool. the halsey lyric: "i want a beautiful ▮▮▮'s despondent laughter." not anymore. i want to wear teal pants my grandmother loves & my cousin's blue flannel & follow her under an overpass, crouched low under roaring concrete. you loved my docs when i first bought them; now i'm planting my feet in tiny rivers in the dark, entering a maze of colorful tunnels & it's been 40 days since i've texted, seen, touched you. i see silvia's tag in bright blue—▮▮▮▮▮—you'd get it, you'd love it, & yet, & yet.

▮▮ i am thinking about the stories we wrote together as i straighten to stand in the light of my headlamp's beam. *luxury ahead* is written on a ceiling overhang. i am thinking of my characters, of *the poppy house,* that which i told you i must rewrite over & over to heal myself. that which i told you i must rewrite so it is all *mine.*

a pink mushroom. a red-lipsticked girl blowing swirling, black & white smoke. coral & turquoise & sapphire-blue cat whiskers. the tunnels echo. like all the things you said & didn't say to me. danielle, beloved protagonist, picks up graffiti in the sequel—we coined that idea together, sitting in the dark on a civic center picnic table, where you held me, bent over the peeling paint, where we ate sushi & cranberry bread i made for us. ███████████████

███████ i went to a real anarchist mutual aid house on tuesday night. you said you didn't know anything about the chamomile collective story-thread i wrote into the most recent *poppy house* draft. did you ever really want to learn? two years ago, i called you the softest, safest space to freedom dream with. ███████████

████████████████ that feels like a fucking joke now. the shelter you were was always going to decay. didn't i build it mostly from scraps? but why, sweetheart, babe, dude, why do i keep talking to myself this way? you haven't been answering questions like that for a long time now. maybe i built the shelter, or maybe you did & neglected to tell me you couldn't hold it up. or maybe you tried to tell me, over & over, but i couldn't hear it, i couldn't hear it, because then, then, the pain would be greater than any mold or water damage. & ██████ said, *you're thinking you're sustaining yourself but in reality you're just starving.* & when did decay creep into letting yourself accept the shelter *i* was for *you?* at least you bought the book with that poem in it. at least i got to tell you: *"shelter/decay" has been nominated for a best of the net award.*

silvia is spraying careful letters, a eulogy for a murdered forest defender, fury at a system that is nothing but a death machine. *r.i.p. tortuguita. fuck 12.* the world outside is seven hundred kinds of disaster, but for now, i am content. i used to be terrified you'd think you were better off without me, but maybe—i am the one better off.

i shake a can of purple spray paint. almost the color my hair was last june. i write *harlow* clumsily on the concrete wall. another of the characters we loved so well. loud voices ricochet from somewhere unseen. we keep moving. high on adrenaline & so, so far away from northwestern michigan. ███████████████████████

silvia is scrawling *sex change <3* in a sliver of empty space & i feel nothing like the people i'm supposed to call colleagues, nothing like those who believe a problem can be solved solely within the system that created it, nothing like those content to remain within that system. nothing like any of those who fled the homeschooled church with you & i, nothing like those who keep themselves isolated & hardened. i think a piece of my soul might die if i have to return to the town where all of that cycles around itself in a potholed, fluorescent purgatory. & i want, i want, & i want to go to ████████ & oregon & ████████. & ██████████ & ███████.

i've been thinking about the stereotype of midwesterners being private, polite. read: closed off, avoidant of what's really hard & matters most. i've been thinking about care & lesbianism & the real meaning of the fluidity & expansiveness of queer relationality. i've been learning how to believe i am not a nuisance or a burden. remember how i was supposed to fly to see silvia & anna before the time of illness struck? how when i got the tickets i was barely out of the closet, a girl hero-worshiping other girls who don't know what they're doing either. but remember when they were the first people you knew who were ████████████████████████████████████ ████████████████? if i'd gone then, i would've texted you the whole time—a girl unable to live in the moment, a girl filtering her life through her best friend, her longed-for ██████████████████, or maybe just ████████, someone to come home to & be understood by. or maybe just wanting to share her life with someone who responded.

but it's different now & i am glad it is *now* that i am here, after silvia left & returned to this city, vesper round & spritely & immortalized in blue whiskers, her lover still here, their dog still here. this is always my family. running through tunnels, angry with america & not keeping all the secrets, not like your family does. i don't want to share my family with you anymore. ████████████████████████ ██████████████ i shake the purple paint can & write in careful lowercase: *empathy is not a luxury.* words my grandfather gave me when i told him about you. maybe someone else living on scraps will see it.

when i show silvia, her pride feels soft like her cat's belly. it's easy to leap up her hand onto the next level of concrete, back toward the entry point. i can hear what you'd text if i showed you pictures— *yooo that's cool as fuck.* but i won't. i'm so far away from the girl who stopped wearing color. bright poppy shirt, green tea sweater. so deeply ██████████████. the ache in my chest; fuck 12; eating spicy beans in a dark, string-lit yard full of anarchists with cold hands; standing under the stars with a joint in my hand; vesper in my lap. ██████████████████████████ do not worry about me.

these things are no longer wild rebellions or miracles. they are simply my life. not grasping, not tiny adrenalines. tonight i will fall asleep in a shirt that says *safe passage.* safe passage. safe passage across this next chapter of life, of *the poppy house,* without you.

we emerge from the tunnels.

ABOUT THE CONTRIBUTORS

- ❖ **Allison Thung** (she/her) is a Singaporean poet. She is the author of *Reacquaint* (*kith books*, 2024), *Molar* (*kith books*, 2024), and *Things I can only say in poems about/to an unspecified 'you'* (*Hem Press*, 2025). Find her at @poetrybyallison or www.allisonthung.com.

- ❖ **Amita Basu** is a Pushcart-nominated writer whose fiction has appeared in over 70 venues including *The Penn Review*, *Bamboo Ridge*, *Jelly Bucket*, *Phoebe*, and *Funicular*. Her debut, *At Play and Other Stories*, is due out with Bridge House Press in 2025.

- ❖ **Anam Tariq** (she/her) writes from India. She is the author of the poetry collection *A Leaf upon a Book* (Leadstart, 2022). Her poems nestle in *The Punch Magazine*, *nether Quarterly*, *Lucky Jefferson*, *Last Leaves*, *Free Verse Revolution*, and elsewhere. Find her at www.anamtariq.in or @anam.tariq_ (IG)

- ❖ **Andrea Aldrete** is a published author from a small Texas border town. She is a mother of two small children, and a wife to an amazing husband. She is a recovering alcoholic that lives a sober life creating cherished memories with her beautiful family.

- ❖ **andrea lianne grabowski** (she/her) is a midwestern lesbian writer occupying Anishinaabe land. her work lives in *fifth wheel press, manywor(l)ds,* and other homes. you can find her on long drives inspired by music, or peering in abandoned windows.

- ❖ **Annabelle Guihan Larsen** is a writer from Chicago. Her fiction has appeared in, *EcoTheo Review* and *New Rivers Press* among other publications,. Her work has been supported by The Elizabeth George Foundation and the Ucross Foundation.

- ❖ **Audric Adonteng** (he/him) is a Ghanaian-American poet. His poetry can be found in *Polyphony Lit Magazine*, *The Empty Inkwell Review*, *The Eunoia Review*, and more. Audric relives small town experiences and brings them to life with his poetic voice.

- ❖ **Bleah Patterson** (she/her) is a queer, southern poet born and raised in Texas. Her work explores contention between identity and home and has been featured in *Electric Literature, Write or Die, Phoebe Literature,* and *Taco Bell Quarterly* and elsewhere.

- ❖ **Caitlin Annette Johnson** (she/they) is a nonbinary poet, novelist, and artist originally from the Deep South. Johnson's newest project, *Empress in Reverse*, explores queer motherhood and all its fun and devastating peculiarities.

- ❖ **Cimmerian Urbanek** is a poet and educator with a focus on environmental issues and disability rights. Her works have been featured in *ArLiJo, In the Margins, Awakenings, Bombay Gin,* and *The Bennington Review.*

- ❖ **Dean Hel** (they/them) is a writer based in Houston, Texas. Their work has appeared or is forthcoming in *Assignment Literary Magazine, Five on the Fifth, Porcupine Literary, Five Minutes,* and *Press Pause Press.* They are at work on a novel.

- ❖ **Divya Venkat Sridhar** (she/her) is an Indian poet raised in Switzerland. Her work has been published by the *Poetry Society, Rattle Magazine, Zindabad Zine*, and more. When she isn't writing, you'll find her singing the La La Land soundtrack (terribly).

- ❖ **Emma Wells** is a mother and English teacher. She has poetry published with various literary journals and magazines. She writes flash fiction, short stories and novels. She is currently writing her sixth novel. Emma won Wingless Dreamer's Bird Poetry Contest of 2022 with 'Carbonito de Sophie' and her short story entitled 'Virginia Creeper' was selected as a winning title by WriteFluence Singles Contest in 2021. Recently, she won Dipity Literary Magazine's 2024 Best of the Net Nominations for Fiction with her short story entitled 'The Voice of a Wildling'. Her poem 'Rose-Tainted was the winner of the poetry category, Discourse Literary Journal, February 2024 Issue. She was shortlisted for her flash fiction writing, 'Agnes Richter', by Anthology. Her first poetry collection entitled 'Reasons to...Evolve' was published in April 2024.

- ❖ **Eugenie Carabatsos** (she/her) is a playwright and occasional poet. Her poetry has been published in *SWWIM, BarBar, Pink Panther, Hare's Paw*, and *1922 Review*. For her theater work, check out New Play Exchange or www.eugeniecarabatsos.com. When she's not writing, she teaches at Dartmouth College.

- ❖ **Georgie Contreras** (she/her) is a Latine writer raised and residing in the Boston area. Her poetry has been published in *The Ana* and *Loud Coffee Press*. You'll usually find her journaling or watching an indie wrestling match from the mid-2000's.

- ❖ **Giselle Linder** (she/her) is an Australian-born artist currently based in Paris, France. Her debut poetry collection, 'City Gothic', was published last year by *Dark Thirty Poetry Publishing*.

- ❖ **Ivy L. James** (she/her) wrote her first story on Post-it notes as a child. Since then, she has graduated to regular paper and enjoys writing queer romance and poetry. Ivy lives in Maryland with her wife. Connect with her at www.authorivyljames.com.

- ❖ **J M Roberts** (she/her) is a writer living in Austin, TX. She was previously published as a Top Issue Finalist by the *Wingless Dreamer Publisher* and *The Closed Eye Open*. She works as a writing intern for the world-renowned Austin Film Festival.

- ❖ **Jessica Swanson** (she/her) is a librarian and a writer. She has had work published with Healthline Zine, and others. She has a fondness for cats, cheese, and fancy tea leaves. Find her on Instagram at everystupidstar and Twitter at Cooljazsheepie.

- ❖ **John Eric Hamel** lives in Oregon. He has published several poems and translations (*Arion, Notre Dame Review, Atlanta Review, American Journal of Poetry*).

- ❖ **Jong Yun Won** (he/him) is a Korean-Canadian currently living in Philadelphia. He studied Creative Writing and English at the University of British Columbia which he paid for by tree planting during the summer. You can find him on Twitter @jjjongwwwon

- ❖ **Katie Beswick** (she/her) is a writer from south east London. Recent poems appear in *Ink Sweat & Tears; Dust Poetry Magazine; Harpy Hybrid; English; Ballast* and *The Citron Review*, among others. Her chapbook is *Plumstead Pram Pushers* (Red Ogre 2024).

- ❖ **Katrin Hessa** (she/her) has a professional background in bioscience research and is currently a PhD student in Melbourne. She has written short stories for online magazines primarily to raise funds for charities such as the UNHCR.

- ❖ **Krystle Eilen** (she/her) is a poet currently attending university. Her works have been featured in *Eunoia Review, A Thin Slice of Anxiety, BlazeVOX, Poetry Life and Times, ZiN Daily*, and *Literary Heist* among others.

- ❖ **Layne Joy Ruda** (she/her) is a Chicago born writer with her MA in Writing and Publishing from DePaul University. Her previous poems can be found in *Ink & Nebula* and *Crook & Folly*. Connect with her on Instagram @layne.joy.

- ❖ **Leslie Cooles** (she/her) is an American writer currently living in the English countryside. When not writing, she can be found traveling, talking all things historical, and wrangling two small children.

- ❖ **Liam Chimba** (He/Him) is a graduate of Creative Writing and Philosophy from the University of Chichester. He lives on the East coast of England and enjoys long walks on the beach whilst listening to music.

- ❖ **Linda M. Crate** (she/her) is a Pennsylvanian writer. She has twelve published chapbooks the latest being: *Searching Stained Glass Windows For An Answer* (Alien Buddha Publishing, December 2022).

- ❖ New Yorker and award-winner, **LindaAnn LoSchiavo** (she/her) is a member of British Fantasy Society, HWA, SFPA & The Dramatists Guild. Books in 2024: "Always Haunted: Hallowe'en Poems," "Apprenticed to the Night," "Felones de Se: Poems about Suicide."

- ❖ **Madeline Rosales** (she/her) has won a Gold Key for the Scholastic Art and Writing Awards, and has publications with *The Academy of the Heart and Mind, The WEIGHT Journal,* and *The Odyssey Youth Magazine.* She edits for *Polyphony Lit.*

- ❖ **Marc Meierkort** (he/him) is an Adjunct Professor at Columbia College Chicago, as well as Managing Editor for *Allium, A Journal of Poetry & Prose.* He earned an MFA in Poetry from Columbia in 2022. A Pushcart nominee, he lives in the Chicago area.

- ❖ **Margaret Elysia Garcia** is the author of the short story collection *Graft* (Tolsun Books), the poetry chapbook *Burn Scars* (Lit Kit Collective), and the debut poetry collection the *daughterland poems* (El Martillo Press). She's the co-editor of the forthcoming *Red Flag Warning: Mutual Aid and Survival in California's Fire Country,* to be published by AK Press in June 2025. She's an MFA student at Chapman University.

- ❖ **Matthew Feinstein** (He/Him) is a poet and writer. He holds an MFA in Poetry from Randolph College. His poems have appeared in *HAD, Heavy Feather Review, Inflectionist Review,* and elsewhere. Learn more at www.matthewfeinsteinwriter.com.

- ❖ **Michelle Young** (she/her) is a Venezuelan-Canadian writer humbly located on the unceded territories of the xʷməθkʷəy̓əm (Musqueam), Sḵwx̱wú7mesh (Squamish), and səlilwətaɬ (Tsleil-Waututh) peoples. Her poetry has previously appeared in *amberflora* and is forthcoming in *SAD Mag.* You can find her at michelleyoung.ca

- ❖ **Natalye Childress** (she/her) is a Berlin-based editor, writer, translator, and sad punk whose writing has been nominated for Best of the Net. She has an MA in creative writing, and her poetry appears or is forthcoming *in Farewell Transmission, Sontag Mag, scaffold, Honeyguide, BRAWL,* and elsewhere.

- ❖ **Noll Griffin** (he/him) is a visual artist, writer, and musician based in Berlin, Germany. His first chapbook titled "Tourist Info" is available through Alien Buddha Press. You can find him on Tumblr/Bluesky/Twitter under @nollthere.

- ❖ When **Nona Lea** isn't writing essays on ecocriticism, she/they work on an MFA at Stonecoast. Lea's work has appeared in *Moss Puppy Magazine, Twoheaded Press Zine, Vial of Bones,* and *QLPORYT*. Find more through her linktree: https://linktr.ee/nona_lea

- ❖ **Paris Woodward-Ganz** (he/him) is a queer poet and a college student. He is creative writing editor for The Student Insurgent, a leftist paper. Previous publications include work in *Querencia Press, North Dakota Quarterly*, and *Crow & Cross Keys*.

- ❖ **Sammy Ismet Merabet** (they/she/he) is an Algerian-American poet, born and raised in Southern California. Their poetry experiments with traditional forms to explore contemporary identity and sensuality.

- ❖ **Sarah Blackshaw** (she/her) is a psychologist and writer who lives in the North of England. She can be found on most things as @academiablues, and her website is www.clinpsychsarah.com

- ❖ **Tanisha E. Khan** (she/her) is a Canadian writer. She has an MFA in Creative Writing from the University of Oregon, and her work has appeared in "apart, a year of pandemic poetry and prose". When not writing she's on walks, petting local cats and dogs.

- ❖ **Tohm Bakelas** is a social worker in a psychiatric hospital. He is the author of several collections of poetry, including "Cleaning the Gutters of Hell (Zeitgeist Press, 2023) and "The Ants Crawl in Circles" (Bone Machine, Inc., 2024).

- ❖ **tommy wyatt** (he/they) are synthesizing digital archives, graveyards, and residual hauntings. he's the author of *DITCHLAPSE / [REALLY AFRAID]; So, Who's Courage?; Trick Mirror or Your Computer Screen*; and others.

- ❖ **Travis Stephens** (he/his/him) lives with his family in Los Angeles. A tugboat captain, his book of poetry, "SKEETER BIT & STILL DRUNK" was published by *Finishing Line Press*.

- ❖ **Yuu Ikeda** (she/they) is a Japan based poet and writer. She loves mystery novels, western art, sugary coffee, and Japanese comic "呪術廻戦 (Jujutsu Kaisen)". She writes poetry on her website. https://poetryandcoffeedays.wordpress.com

OTHER TITLES FROM QUERENCIA